# 'Tell me what you want, Tessa.'

Marc's voice, low and husky, whispered over her skin. But even with need growing to fever pitch the words stuck in her throat, blocked by some lingering shyness. She shook her head, her eyes begging him to understand.

'I can't.'

'You must. Tell me what you want me to do.'

She swallowed hard, one part of her hating him.

'I want you,' she whispered. 'I want you to make love to me.'

**Dear Reader**

Hello and welcome once again to Euromance! This month Rachel Elliot takes us to the delightful island of Jersey—an ideal setting for romance, with its unique character and charm. Furthermore the story is set in summer, when the island's attractions are highlighted by the wonderfully warm and sunny weather. So all you have to do is sit back, relax and allow us to transport you across the Channel. . . Enjoy your trip!

*The Editor*


**The author says:**

'Jersey's always struck me as a place of romance—because of its intriguing history and its blend of French and British influences, as well as its glorious scenery—and excellent sunshine record! When I was given the opportunity to write a Euromance, Jersey seemed the perfect venue. It's a fascinating mixture—an important financial centre, yet richly steeped in myth and legend. Just the sort of place where dreams can be born—not to mention love stories!'

*Rachel Elliot*


★ TURN TO THE BACK PAGES OF THIS BOOK FOR *WELCOME TO EUROPE*. . .OUR FASCINATING FACT-FILE ★

# LEAP OF FAITH

BY
RACHEL ELLIOT

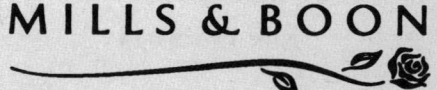

MILLS & BOON LIMITED
ETON HOUSE, 18–24 PARADISE ROAD
RICHMOND, SURREY, TW9 1SR

**DID YOU PURCHASE THIS BOOK WITHOUT A COVER?**

If you did, you should be aware it is **stolen property** as it was reported *unsold and destroyed* by a retailer. Neither the Author nor the publisher has received any payment for this book.

*All the characters in this book have no existence outside the imagination of the Author, and have no relation whatsoever to anyone bearing the same name or names. They are not even distantly inspired by any individual known or unknown to the Author, and all the incidents are pure invention.*

*All Rights Reserved. The text of this publication or any part thereof may not be reproduced or transmitted in any form or by any means, electronic or mechanical, including photocopying, recording, storage in an information retrieval system, or otherwise, without the written permission of the publisher.*

*This book is sold subject to the condition that it shall not, by way of trade or otherwise, be lent, resold, hired out or otherwise circulated without the prior consent of the publisher in any form of binding or cover other than that in which it is published and without a similar condition including this condition being imposed on the subsequent purchaser.*

*MILLS & BOON and the Rose Device are trademarks of the publisher.*

*First published in Great Britain 1994 by Mills & Boon Limited*

© Rachel Elliot 1994

*Australian copyright 1994   Philippine copyright 1994 This edition 1994*

ISBN 0 263 78579 3

*Set in 10 on 12 pt Linotron Times 01-9408-51028*

*Typeset in Great Britain by Centracet, Cambridge Made and printed in Great Britain*

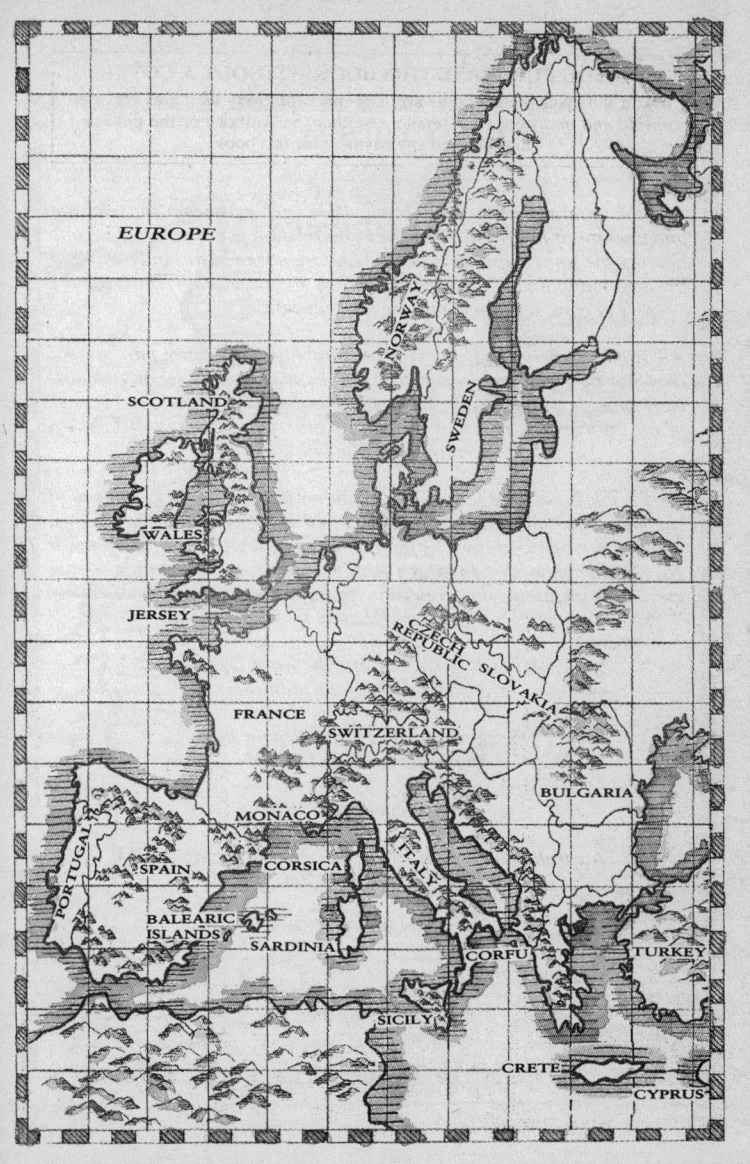

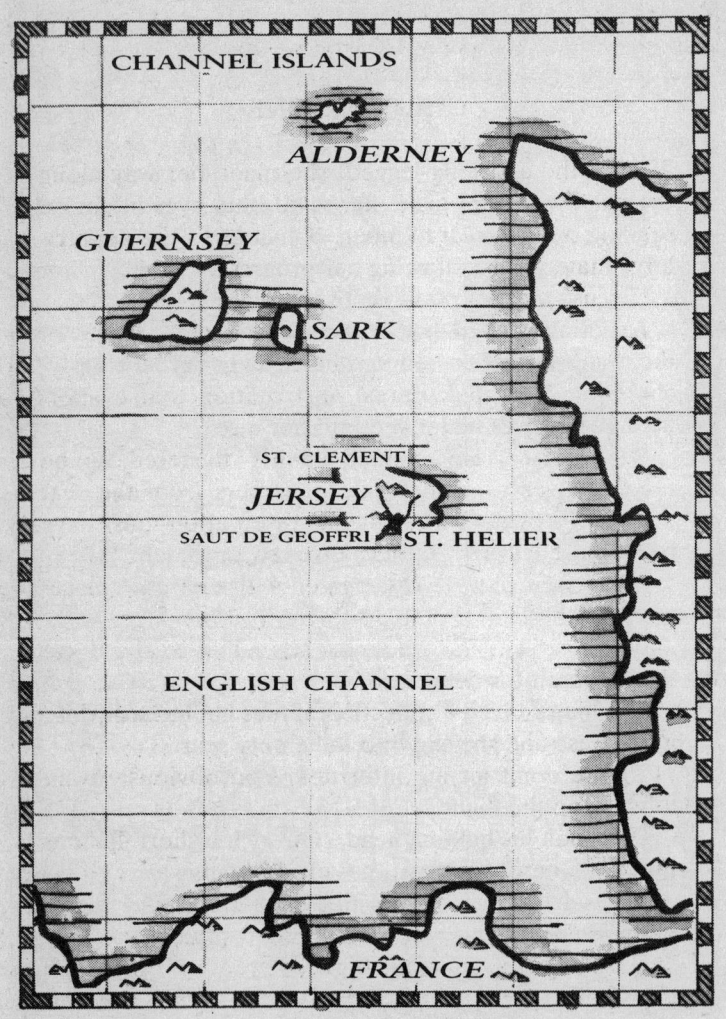

# CHAPTER ONE

TALL, lithe and long-legged, she made her way along the narrow central aisle, her vivid blue eyes intent on seeking out her seat number, oblivious to the appreciative male stares following her progress.

'Excuse me? I believe that's my place.'

Irritation glinted briefly behind the thick lenses of the man's glasses as he lifted his head to reveal elderly, somewhat cynical features, an irritation that evaporated instantly as he looked into her face.

'Of course.' He seemed faintly flustered as he reached over to clear a pile of papers from the seat next to his own. 'I thought this reservation must have been cancelled. If you'll just give me a moment.'

'Take your time.' Tessa smiled with tolerant amusement as the man scrabbled to retrieve his paperwork, and almost sent the whole lot cascading to the floor. 'It's my fault for being late.'

The man shoved a collection of files haphazardly into a briefcase and she slid into the empty seat.

'Please don't let me interrupt. You obviously want to work on the flight.'

He shook his balding head. 'On such a short flight as this, it's hardly worth the effort. Anyway...' his expression held the suggestion of a leer '...I didn't know I'd be having such stimulating company.'

Tessa suppressed a faint sigh. There were times, and this looked like being one of them, when she was inclined to wish the gods hadn't been quite so generous in their gifts to her. This man was old enough to be her father — and then some — but her presence had apparently given him a whole new lease of life. Right now all she wanted was to sit quietly and to take time out to do some hard thinking, but he clearly intended to make the most of the short trip. And that had nothing to do with her personality or character, she acknowledged ruefully. For all he knew, she could be bland, or boring, or even downright unpleasant. He clearly didn't care about that — he was simply drawn to her wide-set aquamarine eyes, and the generously wide mouth that seemed of its own accord to promise sensuous pleasures. And even though her rich honey-blonde hair was now cut in a boyishly short style rather than the waist-length tresses she'd sported most of her life, it still seemed to act as a beacon.

'Is everything all right for you?'

Tessa nodded at the stewardess, recognising without rancour the barely perceptible hostility behind the professional smile. A pretty enough woman in her own right, she was clearly put out by Tessa's presence and the stir she'd created among the other passengers.

'Everything's just fine,' she returned amiably. 'Will we be taking off soon?'

The woman nodded. 'Make sure your seatbelts are fastened. I'm just about to run through the emergency procedures.'

The man at Tessa's side groaned audibly as the stewardess continued along the aisle. 'Lord I get bored with all that rigmarole. The same old spiel every time.'

'You'd be grateful for it if there ever was an emergency,' Tessa pointed out, and he grinned unrepentantly.

'I've done this flight so often I could recite it in my sleep.' His pale grey eyes scrutinised her speculatively. 'What about you? Have you ever been to Jersey before?'

She shook her head. 'Never.'

He patted her hand comfortably. 'Well, if this is your first flight, don't worry about a thing. I'll be happy to look after you.'

She managed to nod solemnly, then was forced to look away, afraid he might see the mirth dancing in her eyes. In truth Jersey was one of the very few places in the world she hadn't visited, and as for flying, the last few years had almost made her more at home on a plane than on the ground. But she wasn't about to get into all of that with him.

'Anyway,' the man went on, blissfully unaware of her amusement, 'we may as well introduce ourselves. I'm Clarke Simpson.'

'Tessa Edwards.' She took his proffered hand, managing only with an effort not to drop it instantly. If there was one thing she hated, it was a limp handshake, and Clarke Simpson's was definitely of the wet-fish variety.

'Are you on holiday?'

'Not exactly,' she hedged.

'A business trip, then? No.' He shook his head. 'You don't look the business type. Though you'd certainly be a wow in the boardroom!' He chuckled heartily at his own wit and she managed to conjure up a weak smile in return. 'I've got it! You're a model, aren't you? I'm sure I've seen you on the front covers of glossy magazines.'

'No. I'm not a model.' She hesitated, unsure just how much she should tell him. Then she gave an imperceptible shrug. The real reason for her trip might be a mystery, even to her, but as far as she knew there was no need to be particularly secretive about it. And if this Clarke Simpson knew Jersey as well as he seemed to imply, she might even pick up some useful information from him. At this stage anything would help.

'I'm going to see a friend of mine,' she said carefully. 'Ralph Duval.'

His genial smile vanished instantly. 'Ralph Duval?' he said sharply. 'Brother to that pirate Marc Duval?'

Almost despite herself she had to smile at the description. She'd heard Ralph use others, none of them as exciting. 'That's correct,' she affirmed.

Clarke Simpson's pale eyes seemed to be regarding her in a whole new light given this information. 'Well, well,' he said, and something in his tone made her shiver slightly.

As the plane started to taxi down the runway, Tessa strove to sound nonchalant. 'In what way is Marc Duval a pirate?'

Clarke pursed his thin lips in a soundless whistle. 'The man's just like his ancestors were before him. Utterly ruthless and utterly without morals.'

Tessa felt a faint tremor of unease.

'He swoops on the weak and defenceless,' Clarke continued grimly. 'Buys up failing businesses to boost his own ever increasing empire. And. . .' the pale eyes turned icy cold as he turned to look at her '. . .he won't hesitate to stab a so-called friend in the back. As I should know.'

Tessa bit her lip. There was something about the man she instinctively didn't like, yet she couldn't help but be alarmed by his grim words. Then she gave herself a mental shake. It wasn't Marc she was going to see. It was Ralph — and he was a million miles removed from the things Clarke had said about his brother.

'Has Ralph followed Marc into the family business, then?' Clarke slid her a calculating look.

She frowned. 'I'm not really sure,' she admitted. She found it hard to imagine Ralph in the shark-infested waters his brother seemed to command so mercilessly, but then she hadn't seen him in some time, and even though he wrote regularly his letters were generally full of light, amusing trivia. Which made his most recent communication all the more puzzling.

'Just be careful in your dealings with that family,' Clarke said abruptly. 'They're not to be trusted.'

To her relief he picked up his briefcase then, and started rummaging through the papers, quite clearly signalling that the conversation was at an end. That suited her just fine. Admittedly she held no loyalty towards Marc — how could she, when she'd never even met the man? — but still, he was Ralph's brother, and she didn't enjoy hearing the Duval name criticised so harshly.

She settled back into her seat with a sigh, feeling a faint pang of longing for her tiny and remote but much-loved cottage deep in the heart of the Scottish borders. She'd only arrived back there in the early hours of the morning, jet-lagged from the long trip back from

Tasmania, wanting nothing more than to close the door behind her and sleep in the comfortable big old bed for a week, sorely needing to recharge her tired batteries before setting off on the next expedition. Ralph's letter had put paid to that idea.

She hadn't even intended to check through the mountain of mail that had accumulated in her absence, feeling nothing could be so important it couldn't wait till she'd caught up on at least a fraction of the sleep she'd been missing. Then she'd spotted Ralph's unmistakable writing and put thoughts of rest on hold, revitalised by the prospect of one of his long, newsy, wickedly amusing letters. Ten minutes later she'd been reaching for the phone to book this flight, and it seemed she'd been on the move ever since.

Ralph Duval. An affectionate, faintly anxious smile touched her lips as his familiar features swam before her mind's eye. He was probably the only person she knew who could simply make her down everything and run — even though she knew perfectly well she'd probably find there was no emergency at all when she reached him. Knowing Ralph's love of the dramatic as she did, she was pretty sure he'd have wildly overstated the urgency of it all. But he'd asked for her help and she'd give it, no matter what it took. After all, he'd been there for her when she most needed a friend, and she certainly wasn't about to turn her back on him now.

Besides which — as much as she might tell herself Ralph was simply playacting again — she couldn't shake the nagging feeling of apprehension that had been dogging her ever since she'd first read his letter. Just what sort of help could he need? And why was it so imperative that she go to Jersey? Why couldn't he simply have spelled it all out in the letter?

The questions were still plaguing her as she followed Clarke off the plane into the small but busy and bustling main hall of Jersey Airport. He bade her farewell with little more than a curt nod, and she found herself wondering about that too. Heaven knew, she hadn't particularly wanted to cultivate any greater depth of friendship with the man — but considering how fulsome he'd been at first, such coolness now seemed extraordinary. It was a coolness that had begun with the mention of the Duval name, she realised — or, more accurately, with the mention of Marc Duval's name.

Then she shrugged her shoulders. She couldn't deny feeling more than a touch intrigued about the elder Duval, with his piratical reputation, but she was here on the island of Jersey to see Ralph — and to help him sort out whatever tangle he'd landed himself in this time. It wouldn't be the first time he'd landed himself in hot water, she thought with a fond grin. The most recklessly generous and open-handed person she'd ever met, he was also a complete sucker at times, with a total inability to say no to anyone. He'd probably become ensnared by yet another wily female with pound signs in her eyes. Though that was hardly fair, she mentally chastised herself — he was a good-looking man, certainly attractive enough to appeal to women in his own right without the added benefit of the family fortune.

It was ironic really that they'd first met when she'd been suffering the first heartbreak of her life, she mused as she hefted her rucksack into a more comfortable position on her shoulders. She'd been in her first year at university when she'd met and been completely bowled over by Dan, an infinitely more sophisticated and experienced postgraduate student. Hugely flattered by his attentions, she had taken some months to realise he had a real taste for wide-eyed freshers — the more naïve, the better. By that time she'd been head over heels in love with him, and finding him wrapped in another girl's arms at a party had devastated her. She smiled ruefully, remembering the way she'd bolted from the party, racked with sobs, only to cannon straight into Ralph.

Stranger though he was to her than, he'd been wonderful, tucking her under his arm and marching her away to a late-night coffee-bar, refusing to let her move till she'd poured out the whole sorry tale. That had been just the start of their friendship, she remembered as she walked across to the taxi rank. The only daughter in a family crammed full of sons, she'd always been more at home in the company of males than females, and Ralph had become yet another brother to her, his fecklessness somehow bringing out the protectiveness in her own soul. Even though he'd been the one to offer comfort in the first place, she'd soon recognised the lost little boy beneath the devil-may-care exterior, and he in his turn had been drawn to her strength and compassion. As her mother had announced with amused resignation after meeting Ralph for the first time, he was simply the latest in the long line of waifs and strays Tessa had taken care of over the years — though he was actually the first human on the list. The others had all been furred or feathered.

'Where to, miss?'

Tessa smiled, hearing the faint traces of an accent in the taxi driver's voice. She already knew from the many hours she'd spent listening to Ralph talk about his beloved home that the island was an intriguing mix of French and English influences—hardly surprising given that it was just fourteen miles from France—but that it stubbornly maintained its own character, and indeed a measure of self-government.

Leaning forward, she gave the driver the address. 'I believe it overlooks a bay if that's any help,' she said.

It was the driver's turn to grin. 'So do many places on Jersey, miss,' he said. 'But don't worry. You're going to the Duval home, yes? I know exactly where that is.'

He proved to be an excellent guide, driving slowly along the sparklingly beautiful sweep of St Brelade's Bay on the south side of the island, which he told her was one of the most popular tourist haunts. Impatient as she was to reach Ralph, she couldn't help but be entranced by the sight of the gloriously golden sands, and the sun glinting on the blue water of the sea. Then it was on through the hustle and bustle of the island's capital of St Helier.

'If you think it's busy now, you should be here in a few weeks' time for our Battle of Flowers,' he told her when she exclaimed over the surprising amount of traffic crawling along the waterfront nose-to-tail. 'You must surely have heard of the Battle, yes? It's world-famous—and truly a sight to be seen. So many incredible creations, and all made entirely from flowers. You will be here for the parade?'

'I'm afraid not,' she said with genuine regret, her

imagination intrigued by the pictures he was painting for her. 'I expect I'll only be staying a couple of days.'

'Perhaps your host will change your mind.' The smile was evident in his tone, even though she could only see the back of his head. 'Marc Duval is well known for his persuasive ways! Not only in business matters, you understand, but also with the ladies.'

'It's not Marc I'm going to see,' Tessa supplied unthinkingly. 'It's his brother, Ralph.'

The man's shoulders lifted in an expressive shrug. 'Ah, yes. The young playboy of the family. I've heard he's a nice young man.'

Tessa pondered that in silence for a moment, chewing absent-mindedly on her bottom lip. It was strange that the comment should have sounded so dismissive — and yet in a way it made sense. She'd always been aware that Ralph felt inferior to his brother. He'd never said as much, of course, but it didn't take a psychiatrist to spot the tell-tale signs in his character. Now she was beginning to understand why — he'd grown up in the shadow of a powerful and charismatic individual, so perhaps it had been inevitable. She'd heard the note of admiration tinged with envy in the driver's voice when he'd spoken of Marc — and it had been completely missing when he'd mentioned Ralph. She felt a twist of compassion for her friend — and yet couldn't help but be aware of a growing sense of intrigue over the elder Duval. Then she shrugged — she probably wouldn't even meet him, so there was little point in speculating.

'This is where we turn off,' the driver turned his head slightly to address her. 'The house is at the end of quite a long drive. You can't see it from the road.'

'Drop me here,' she requested impulsively. 'I could do with the chance to stretch my legs.'

'But your luggage?' He pursed his lips doubtfully. 'It is quite a long walk if you're encumbered.'

'No matter,' she returned cheerfully. 'My shoulders are quite accustomed to the weight of a rucksack.'

Which was no less than the truth, she mused as she set off along the drive, after giving the driver a farewell wave. She'd walked a lot of miles with a pack on her back, searching out the locations and the creatures she'd then spend long hours photographing. And she was practically an expert in the art of putting up tents — though, come to think of it, the first time she'd done it had been on a camping trip with Ralph. He'd been completely useless, she remembered now with a wry grin. Not that she'd really expected anything else, since practical matters had never been his strong suit. She'd been amazed she'd even been able to persuade him to go on something as lacking in luxury as a camping trip, knowing his love of comfort. When she asked why he'd agreed, his answer was a surprise.

'Because I can't wait to see the look on Marc's face when I tell him.' His grin was endearingly schoolboyish, an image further compounded by the lock of dark brown hair that would insist on flopping over his forehead no matter how many times he raked it back with his long, slender fingers. 'It is my favourite sport in life after all — trying to see if I can crack those dark, saturnine features of his into a smile.'

'And you think this will do it?'

He sent her a wryly self-mocking look. 'Surely any creature with the remotest sense of humour would be forced to laugh at the sight of me in hiker's shorts with a rusksack on my back and a billy-can swinging from my shoulder!'

'True,' she conceded with a grin. 'But is that really what you want? To have him laughing at you?'

His megawatt smile dimmed. 'It would make a change from having him glower all the time.'

'Aren't you being a bit unfair,' she'd probed gently, knowing from countless conversations just how much in awe he was of his older brother. Coming from a large, noisy and thoroughly irreverent brood herself, the relationship had always seemed a strange one. She loved, adored and even respected her brothers, but she certainly didn't quake in her shoes at the very thought of them, as Ralph seemed to do whenever he mentioned Marc's name.

'Unfair?' He seemed to examine the word, then shook his head. 'No, I don't think so. You'd have to meet him to really understand. He's a hard man—well, I suppose he's had to be really,' he added with the sense of fairness she'd always liked in him. 'Marc was just eighteen when our parents died in a car crash, and I was all of ten. He had a hell of a fight on his hands persuading the authorities he was a responsible enough character to take on my upbringing. And then of course he had the family business to contend with as well. Lesser men would have cracked under the strain of it all—or simply thrown up their hands and refused to have anything to do with it.'

'Do you think he was ever tempted to do that?'

'Marc?' He shot her an incredulous look. 'It would never even have occurred to him. The family has always meant too much to him—we can trace our roots right back to William the Conquerer, you know. He'd never have lain down and let some usurper walk in and take over what our forebears built up. He's intensely proud and just as intensely possessive. When something belongs to Marc, he won't ever let it go.'

'Including you?' she hazarded softly.

He nodded bleakly. 'Correct.'

Pushing herself with an effort back to the present, Tessa gave a faint sigh as she saw the driveway stretching ahead of her, and as yet no signs of the house. Feeling a faint sheen of perspiration break out on her forehead as she walked along beneath a glowingly hot sun, she gave in to temptation and veered to the right, spotting an enormous old tree with huge spreading branches, offering shade. As fit and healthy as she was, still the last few days had taken their toll, and it would take some time before she fully recovered from the rigours of the last trip, not to mention the jet-lag still dogging her.

Shrugging the backpack from her shoulders, she sat down with her back to the tree, and fished in the pocket of her shorts for Ralph's letter, now somewhat crumpled. She'd read it umpteen times over the past hours, but no matter how hard she tried, she couldn't make sense of it.

> 'Darling Tessa, Come and intercede for my threatened soul. He wants me to sell it to the devil — she wants me to strive for purer, higher ideals. I'm being torn in two. Help!

He hadn't bothered to sign his name, but he hadn't needed to. She'd have known his writing and his melodramatic style anywhere. But what did it all mean?

Who was he talking about — and what was all that nonsense about his soul?

She sat for a few moments longer, enjoying the cool of the shade, then got to her feet with a faintly regretful sigh, brushing leaves and bits of soil from her legs. Though she rarely gave her own appearance more than a passing thought, it did occur to her that the outfit of shorts, walking boots and a sleeveless denim shirt probably wasn't the most appropriate for an encounter with the redoubtable Marc Duval, but there was no real reason to expect she'd actually meet him. She knew he kept his base on his island home, but his multifarious dealings took him all over the world. He was probably abroad on a business trip somewhere — or at least holed up in a boardroom, embroiled in a red-hot and acrimonious takeover.

She paused in the act of slinging her camera gear round her neck, surprised to discover she'd actually be disappointed rather than relieved to miss out on meeting him. Ridiculous though it seemed, there was a part of her that wanted to see him, just once. Must be the same part which kept urging her on to capture wild animals on film, she thought with a grin. He was an enigma — a challenge. And, if Ralph was to be believed — every bit as dangerous as any wild animal.

Strangely enough, this was the first time Ralph had ever invited her to visit his home — if his letter could be seen as an invitation. She frowned at the thought, then shook her head. The mystery would soon be cleared up. If he was at home. She'd tried to telephone him from the airport, only to be informed by a woman's voice that Ralph Duval wasn't available.

She shrugged off a faint but nagging feeling of

apprehension. If he wasn't sitting round waiting for her call, she had only herself to blame. She should have contacted him to tell him she was on her way—instead she'd acted in her usual impulsive way, and simply hit the road all over again. Well, it was a beautiful day—he was probably toasting happily on one of the island's many beautiful beaches, soaking up the sun.

She carried on walking for a few moments more, then as she turned a corner in the twisting drive, she was stopped in her tracks by the sight of the most beautiful house she'd ever seen. Set amongst trees, built from granite as she knew many island homes were, and fronted by a granite archway, it seemed to radiate a kind of serenity, in the way of old monasteries and convents. Almost unconsciously she reached for her camera, dropping to her knees as she automatically scanned the sky for the position of the sun.

For the moment her mission on the island was entirely forgotten, her every thought centred on capturing the building on film. It was far removed from the wildlife she'd made her own speciality, yet the house seemed to call out to the photographer in her soul, making her oblivious to everything else as she prowled around, taking shot after shot. At last she lowered the camera with a happy sigh, only to freeze in utter disbelief as a heavy hand thudded down on to her shoulder.

'What the hell do you think you're doing?'

## CHAPTER TWO

'THERE'S really no need. . .' Tessa tried to twist round to face her captor, but the hand on her shoulder kept her facing firmly frontwards. 'Look,' she tried again, striving to sound reasonable, 'if I'm trespassing, I do apologise, but. . .'

'Who are you working for?' A male voice barked the question several inches above her left ear, and almost despite herself she was impressed and a little intimidated. Since she was tall by any standards, not many men towered over her by that much. Trust her to fall into the clutches of a giant. And an unfriendly one at that.

'Working for?' She frowned uncomprehendingly. 'What's that got to do. . .?'

'Which rag.' He bit out impatiently. 'Which piece of gutter-filth? Which tabloid trash-merchant?'

'Oh!' As confusion cleared, she smiled. 'You think I'm paparazzi? Nothing could be further from the truth. I'm a wildlife photographer — I specialise in endangered species.'

The man gave a disbelieving grunt. 'You were expecting to find the odd snow leopard beneath the trees? Or an orang-utan?'

She grimaced, realising her claim must sound pretty ridiculous under the circumstances. 'No, of course not. What I meant to say is that I'm *usually* a wildlife photographer.'

'And what are you today?' The voice held no suggestion that its owner was even remotely amused, and she sighed inwardly. It would have helped immeasurably if her captor had possessed a sense of humour, but that seemed a forlorn hope.

She shrugged in what she could only hope would pass for a nonchalant manner. 'I'm not anything in particular,' she said lightly. 'I spotted the house and thought it looked nice, so I decided to take a few quick shots. But actually I'm here to see a friend.'

'His name?'

A fleeting moment of rebellious mischief made her consider challenging his automatic assumption that her friend was male, but she dismissed it. This was not the time to play games.

'Ralph Duval,' she said calmly.

'I've heard enough,' the voice said. 'You're coming with me.'

'Coming where?' Instinct told her it would be better to simply obey, and she was perfectly capable of taking instruction, but his autocratic, dictatorial manner was really getting under her skin, making her bridle. Just who did he think he was anyway? 'I'm going nowhere.' She planted her feet firmly on the earth, bracing herself.

'Then we'll both stay here. Till you change your mind.'

Even though she was normally very easy-going, Tessa nevertheless possessed a well-developed stubborn streak. However something told her she was a callow beginner in the art of intractability in comparison with this man. She brazened it out for a few heavily silent minutes, than gave in with a exclamation of disgust.

'Oh, for goodness' sake! All right, then—I'll go with you if it's so all-fired important to you.'

'Just head towards the house.' There was no trace of triumph in his voice, and for some unaccountable reason that just riled her all the more. He'd won, hadn't he? Surely any normal person wouldn't have been able to resist the temptation to crow—just a little? But then he apparently wasn't an ordinary person—she hadn't even seen him yet, she reminded herself incredulously—but she didn't need to see him to know he was powerful. His very aura told her that.

'Look,' she tried again, 'this really is unnecesssary. If you'd just let me explain.'

'Keep walking.'

With an audibly pained sigh, she did as she was told, even though it infuriated her beyond belief to meekly obey. As she walked towards the house she mentally listed all the grisly retributions she could happily wreak, starting with staking him out over a convenient ant-hill, but dismissing each one as far too gentle.

As they reached the granite archway of the beautiful old building, it was with a sense of great relief that she spotted a middle-aged woman walking towards them, her expression faintly curious.

'Excuse me,' Tessa called out, 'I wonder if you could possibly convince this gentleman to let me go. He appears to be holding me captive.' She switched on her brightest, most appealing smile, but the woman simply slanted a questioning glace at the man behind her.

'Perhaps you didn't hear me.' Tessa tried again, then bit her lip, belatedly realising the woman might not speak English. This was Jersey after all, an island with strong French connections. Cars might drive on the left, British-style, but every place-name she'd spotted had been in French. '*Parlez-vous français?*' she asked hopefully.

'This lady has come to see Ralph,' the man behind her cut in, his voice calm and unruffled. 'She claims to be a friend.'

The woman raised her eyebrows, then gave Tessa a smile that managed to be both sympathetic and faintly knowing at the same time. 'You called from the airport earlier?'

'Yes, I did.'

'I told you he was unavailable.'

The woman's tone was mild, yet Tessa heard its underlying note of reproof and coloured uncomfortably. Perhaps she should have booked into one of the island's hotels and waited till she could speak to him, instead of simply barging on to the Duval property like this. Really, one of these days she might learn to curb her impulsive nature!

'I know you did,' she returned in a low voice, 'and I'm sorry if I'm being a nuisance turning up out of the blue like this. But it is important that I see Ralph.'

The woman nodded. 'I'm sure it is.' A tiny smile played at the corners of her mouth as she glanced towards the man, then nodded in response to some unspoken message from him. 'Now, why don't you go along into the house. I'll bring you a cool drink.'

'Thank you.' Warmed by the woman's hospitality after the man's unfriendliness, Tessa gave her a grateful smile. The feeling of unease returned however as she walked into the house, and watched the woman walk away along a corridor. Not that it wasn't a beautiful place, she acknowledged silently as she looked curiously about her—not only beautiful, but warm and comfortable too. No, her wariness sprang from a tiny inner voice warning her to tread carefully, that she was entering a lion's den she might never escape from. Then she gave herself a mental shake. She was being ridiculous, letting her imagination run away with her. She was simply the victim of a misunderstanding, that was all. Once Ralph appeared, all would be well.

'We'll go into the library,' the man said curtly. 'Through here.'

She winced inwardly as the heavy oak door swung shut behind them but forced herself to stand perfectly immobile. Not for worlds would she allow him to realise how intensely nervous she'd suddenly become. She heard him moving behind her, but stood her ground, staring resolutely ahead, refusing to give him the satisfaction of turning to look at him.

'Now.' His voice was devoid of emotion. 'Who are you?'

She felt an inane and thoroughly misplaced desire to laugh, and welcomed the sensation, even though she knew it sprang from inner tension. It was strangely reassuring to know her sense of the ridiculous was still intact. It afforded her at least some minor form of defence. Stiffening her spine and planting her feet several inches apart, she grasped her hands behind her back in the manner of a soldier at ease.

'Private Tessa Edwards, sir. And may I be so bold as to ask your name?'

'Very well.' He paused for what seemed like an eternity, and in the almost tangible silence between them, she wondered wildly if he could hear her heart beating a jungle tattoo. 'My name is Marc Duval.'

She heard his words with a faint feeling of inevitability. She should have guessed straight away — probably would have done if she hadn't been so sure he'd be away on business somewhere. Yet who else could it have been? After everything Ralph had told her about his autocratic brother, his behaviour shouldn't even have surprised her. Completely forgetting her earlier resolution, she turned slowly round, her eyes widening to their fullest extent and the blood draining from her cheeks as she came face to face with him for the first time. It was a staggering, mind-blowing moment.

He was like Ralph, she realised dazedly, like him and yet a million miles removed from him. Ralph was tall and slender as a reed — Marc was taller still and powerfully built, a big man, yet carrying not one ounce of excess flesh. Ralph's hair was dark, his eyes a gentle, laughing brown — in essence Marc had the same colouring, yet on him it seemed infinitely more vivid and alive, his hair raven-black, his eyes a piercing, penetrating amber.

Ralph had a permanent air of being relaxed to the point of being languid, but there was nothing even remotely languid about this man. He was like a black panther she'd once seen, curled up in the sun yet watchful, ready to spring. Later she'd seen the panther stalk and claim its prey, horrified yet fascinated by its ruthlessness, its remorselessness in making the kill. Marc Duval would be every bit as ruthless, she realised, feeling her heart sink slowly to her feet. In fact, now that he was standing before her, it was all too easy to believe the claims Clarke Simpson had made on the plane. This man was descended from pirates — and the heritage was clear in the hawklike planes of his uncompromising features.

'Now.' His eyes swept over her, narrowing dangerously. 'What do you want with Ralph?'

She opened her mouth to answer, then closed it again abruptly. Open and honest by nature, she'd been about to launch into the tale of Ralph's letter, but something in Marc's demeanour stopped her, though she wasn't sure exactly what it was. In any case, she rationalised, the whole thing could turn out to be no more than histrionics on Ralph's part. Heaven knew she'd witnessed his love of the theatrical often enough before. Had even found it endearing. Marc Duval would not. So to tell him she was here in answer to a plea for help might do nothing more than make herself — and Ralph — appear foolish.

'I simply came to visit him, that's all,' she said lightly, managing to shrug her shoulders off-handedly.

'Why?'

'Why?' She was dismayed to discover her usual quicksilver wits had deserted her, leaving her mind barren of inspiration. It was still more disconcerting to find she was in severe danger of losing herself in his amber-eyed gaze. It was a sensation she'd never experienced — had never come close to experiencing, even with Dan. She'd only just met this man, for goodness' sake — and on short acquaintance she certainly hadn't found anything to like in his brusque, autocratic manner. Yet here she was, standing before him like a callow schoolgirl, biting her lip and lost for words.

'You seem to be finding it hard to answer. Yet it doesn't strike me as a particularly difficult question.'

Rattled by her own lack of composure, she glared back at him. 'It's not difficult at all. But you're making me feel as if I'm on trial! I don't normally get this sort of reception when I visit a friend.'

'No,' he returned drily. 'I don't imagine you do.' His eyes roamed lazily over her body, making her feel suddenly, strangely vulnerable, and totally underdressed in her skimpy shorts and sleeveless shirt. She'd never been ashamed of her body, but in that moment she'd have given everything she possessed to be enveloped from head to foot in totally concealing black. Preferably with a yashmak for good measure.

She started back in surprise as he took a couple of steps towards her, then tossed her head defiantly as he threw her a wryly questioning look.

'I was about to make myself more comfortable by taking a seat,' he said. 'Why don't you do the same?'

She was about to refuse, then realised she'd be at a psychological disadvantage standing while he was sitting, like a mischievous child sent to the headmaster for punishment. With bad grace she gave a single nod of unwilling acquiescence, and subsided into the armchair he'd pointed to. Unthinkingly she crossed her legs, then fervently wished she hadn't as the move tugged her shorts upwards, revealing still more of her golden-skinned thighs.

'So.' The gleam in his tawny eyes told her he was far from oblivious to the leg show she was affording him, and she was hard-pressed not to wriggle in the seat from sheer heated embarrassment. 'Perhaps we should start again. How do you know my brother?'

'How do I know him?' She was pained by the question. But as she felt his watching eyes upon her, she schooled her normally all-too expressive features to remain impassive. A poker player she wasn't, but instinct told her it wouldn't be smart to show her cards too early in this game.

She tilted her chin upwards, looking him straight in the eye. 'I've known Ralph since we were at university together,' she said calmly.

'Where?'

'Where?' She blinked, thoroughly taken aback. 'Don't you know where Ralph took his degree?'

His expression didn't alter. 'Do you?'

He was testing her. Ridiculous as it seemed, he was testing her — checking for proof that she really did know Ralph.

'Aberdeen,' she returned stiltedly. 'Ralph studied English — though not very often.' She offered a hopeful smile in his direction, then let it die away. 'My degree was in zoology.'

He raised one jet-black eyebrow. 'Very different courses,' he commented. 'I'm surprised your paths crossed.'

'They didn't exactly cross as much as collide.' And that was as much as he was going to get of that little story, she decided resolutely. Wild horses wouldn't make her tell this grimly indifferent man about Dan. Even now, long after the heartache had faded away, the memory of that night could still sting. Though it hadn't all been bad of course, since she'd met Ralph. And Marc was right in that they'd probably never have met otherwise.

'Just what sort of relationship do you have with my brother, Miss Edwards?' The amber eyes seemed to bore into her.

'Relationship?' She couldn't help but smile at the question. 'The best kind of relationship—we're...'

'Lovers?'

She flinched. 'No,' she said steadily. 'Not lovers. We're friends. In fact I'd say best friends.'

'Really?' He raised one jet-black eyebrow. 'And yet until today I'd never heard of you.'

She'd been about to make an attempt to explain the kind of affectionate but entirely platonic friendship she shared with Ralph, but the cool brutality of his words slammed into her stomach with the force of a fist. She slumped back into the soft leather of the big old armchair, unconsciously seeking its support.

'Doesn't that strike you as odd, Miss Edwards?' he went on relentlessly. 'Surely in normal circumstances people who are intimate with one another take every opportunity to mention the other's name. Don't they?'

Helplessly Tessa shook her head. 'I'm sure they do. But it isn't like that with us.'

'Don't tell me you're changing your story? You've just told me that you and Ralph are close friends—are you going to backtrack on that?'

She knew from the unpleasant emphasis he placed on the word 'close' that he was twisting her words, and she was powerless to stop him. Angry denials burned in her throat but she bit them back, pride refusing to give him the satisfaction of screaming back at him, much as she wanted to. Underneath the anger there was bitterness too, she realised painfully, a bitterness that could only be aimed at Ralph. Why had he been so secretive—had he been ashamed of their friendship?

Gripped by the thought, she glanced around her, taking in the surroundings properly for the first time since she'd entered the room. The library spoke money — old, long-established money. Being singularly unmaterialistic herself, she knew little and cared less about the trappings of wealth, but she was able to recognise them when she saw them. The room was exquisite, with its wood panelling and fine old period furniture, elegant yet totally without ostentation.

She'd realised at an early stage of knowing Ralph that he came from a moneyed background, and he knew from his many visits to her home that her family, though comfortable, came nowhere near his on the social scale. It hadn't made any difference. Or so she'd believed. But this was the first time she'd been in his home. The first time he'd ever invited her. Had he been afraid she'd disgrace him in the rarefied atmosphere of his own milieu?

'So.' The sound of Marc's voice sliced into her troubled thoughts and she blinked, startled. 'Why have you come here, Miss Edwards?'

'I've already told you.' She glared back at him, her eyes dark with the hurt he'd inflicted so casually. 'To see Ralph.'

'Why now?'

'No particular reason.' She'd never been a good liar, and now to her dismay a betraying heat was rising in her cheeks.

He shook his hard head. 'You disappoint me,' he said obliquely.

She frowned. 'Disappoint you? In what way?'

'I thought you might have come to congratulate Ralph.' His eyes glittered strangely.

'Congratulate him?'

'I believe you heard what I said.' He gave her a

mockingly reproving look. 'Come, come, Miss Edwards. Don't tell me you haven't heard the good news?' He reached down to a rack at his side and selected a glossy magazine. 'Isn't this the real reason for your sudden and unexpected visit?'

Confused, she leaned forward to take the proffered paper, her eyes widening as she found herself looking at a coloured image of Ralph and a girl she'd never seen before. Above the photograph a stark headline speculated, 'Wedding bells to ring for island playboy?'

'Is it true?' She lifted her eyes from the magazine. 'Is Ralph getting married?'

Marc lifted his shoulders fractionally but otherwise ignored the question. Realising he was watching her closely, awaiting her reaction, she leapt to her feet, suddenly too restless to stay in the confines of the armchair. She walked over to the huge bay windows and stared through the glass to the sweeping expanse of gardens beyond. She was pleased for Ralph—when she got used to the idea she'd be overjoyed. But hearing this way, so callously and heartlessly, had pierced her to the heart. If he'd told her his news himself, she'd have flung her arms around him and danced for the sheer sweet delight of it. Hadn't she always told him what he really needed in life was the love of a good woman?

'If you're devising a little plot to prevent the wedding, I'd advise you not to bother.'

Tessa spun round, startled by the sound of his voice at her shoulder. He hadn't made a single sound as he'd crossed the room.

'I haven't the slightest intention. . .'

Ignoring her protest, he raised one hand to cup her

cheek. The touch of his fingers seemed to burn through her skin, making her tremble, yet she was rooted to the spot, incapable of moving.

'Forget it,' he said in a voice that was soft, yet heavy with meaning. 'I know my brother's reputation — and you're not the first disappointed young woman to think she could change his mind about settling down. Though you are the first to actually turn up in person,' he added, with a grim smile. 'The others have been content to make long, tearful telephone calls. But, whatever you may think you had with Ralph, he's lost to you now.'

Angered as much by her own bewildering response to his touch as by his words, she reared away from his hand, glaring furiously back at him.

'You seem very confident of that.'

'I am.' The glint in his amber eyes was steely, making her regret her own impetuous rejoinder, but it was too late to take it back now. Stunned into immobility by his very nearness, she tried to shatter the spell by shaking her head in denial of his insinuations, but he slid his hand to the back of her neck, and the coolly arrogant possession of his touch took her breath away. A tiny voice somewhere deep inside mocked her weakness, but she was helpless, caught up in the thrall of something she'd never known before — something she could only name as physical desire, though the realisation shamed her to the core.

The strength of her response to Marc was all the more shattering since she'd long ago resigned herself to accept that she wasn't and never would be a passionate woman. She'd made that discovery with Dan — oh, she'd enjoyed his kisses and caresses, but they'd lit no fire within her and to his annoyance they'd never left her hungering for more. She could still remember his aggrieved cry when she'd found him with the other woman at the party.

'At least she doesn't flinch away from me every time I touch her,' he'd said bitterly. 'She's got blood in her veins — she's not a pretty but unfeeling doll like you.'

Since then she'd devoted her energies to her career, finding fulfilment in her work instead, aware of a faint wistful curiosity when she saw other couples together, but never tempted to try again with anyone else. With Ralph she'd shared an easy, affectionate relationship. She'd never felt anything but fondness for him, yet she was burning up beneath his brother's casual touch. But how could she possibly desire this hateful man? Even as she wondered, he lowered his head and her lips parted in helpless welcome, as though she no longer held any control over her own body.

The first touch of his mouth made her heart miss a beat, his kiss no caress but a brand burning his mark on to her soft lips. She groaned desperately, caught up in a sudden crazy storm of feeling. For the first time she regretted her lack of physical experience — it might at least have afforded her the armour of familiarity. Instead she was being devoured by an entirely unknown sensation, and had no way of fighting it.

His hands ran over her body, igniting molten rivers in her veins, and unconsciously she arched up towards him, blindly seeking more and still more. Her hands snaked up behind his neck, her fingers driving into his thick black hair as his tongue plundered the sweetness of her mouth. Just a few short moments ago she'd wished she'd been wearing an all-enveloping robe —

now even her skimpy shirt and shorts seemed an unbearable barrier between her skin and his marauding hands. Her nipples, taut and aching, pressed into his chest, her legs moulded against his powerful thighs.

With an angry exclamation he tore his mouth from hers and she gazed up at him in cloudy confusion, her lips still tingling from his kiss.

'I think that proves my theory,' he said grimly, lifting his hands to pull her fingers away from the back of his neck.

'Theory?' She was disorientated, bewildered, thrown completely off-balance.

He nodded, his lips thinning to an angry white line in his tanned face. 'When you rushed so dramatically to the window after hearing of Ralph's forthcoming wedding, I thought about offering you a penny for your thoughts. However, something told me you might be hoping for considerably more. I decided to see for myself if I was correct.'

The insinuation burned into her skin like acid, making the blood drain from her face. 'What do you mean?' Her voice was barely above a whisper.

'Come, Miss Edwards, you're a modern woman. Tough, capable, resourceful.' Even as she shuddered at the undisguised venom in his tone, she found herself marvelling at his ability to make the words seem insulting. 'On admittedly short acquaintance I'd say you're a considerably stronger character than my brother. He must have seemed like a godsend to you — a veritable treasure trove just ripe for plundering.'

'What are you saying?' She could barely force the words past lips grown achingly dry. 'What do you think I am?'

His smile was malevolent. 'I know exactly what you are,' he said silkily. 'Shall I list the adjectives for you? Shrewd, conniving and opportunistic—those should do for starters.' Then he shook his head. 'But I can think of one phrase that sums up all the rest. What you are, Miss Tessa Edwards, is a gold-digging little tramp.'

## CHAPTER THREE

TESSA stared back at him, her blue eyes wide in aghast horror. She was too shocked even for anger, her body trembling.

'How dare you?' Her voice was low and barely controlled. 'You don't know me at all. How can you say such a despicable thing?'

He was unmoved, his expression cold and mocking.

'I've met your kind often enough to recognise them,' he said shortly. 'That's the price a rich man has to pay—all the little bees think they can come buzzing round the honey-pot with impunity.' His lips twisted scornfully. 'I'm perfectly capable of dealing with grasping, greedy women. My brother, alas, is not. He's always been a sucker for a pretty face.'

Infuriatingly, she couldn't even disagree with that. She'd frequently had to bail Ralph out herself, even to resignedly playing the part of the wronged girlfriend when he found himself in yet another situation too hot to handle. He was a good looking man—and famed for his largesse. Since he didn't possess a mean bone in his body, he could never resist a sob story or a wide-eyed appeal. The two things combined made him a perfect target for a certain type of female—but to discover she was now being classed along with them was irony in the extreme. It was also incredibly galling. Ralph would have showered her with gifts if she'd let him, but she'd adamantly refused to accept anything other than silly little novelties or posies.

Taking a deep, steadying breath, she squared up to him. 'You have no right to make such a terrible accusation about me,' she said adamantly. 'And no proof whatsoever.'

'No proof?' His mouth thinned cruelly as he reached out to grasp her wrist, lifting it to eye level. 'This bracelet,' he barked harshly, 'can you deny Ralph gave it to you?'

'I wouldn't even attempt to deny it,' she shot back hotly. 'But it's only a cheap little thing—a trinket.'

Marc Duval's lips curved into a mirthless smile. 'A trinket which has been in my family for more than a hundred years,' he said. 'As to it's being cheap, I could suggest you took it to a jeweller of repute to ascertain its real value. However I'm quite sure you've done that already.'

Tessa eyed the delicate little chain with a mixture of horror and incredulity. She'd been wearing it for so many years, she tended to forget its existence—to discover she'd been sporting a valuable Duval heirloom so casually made her shudder. But more than that, she felt a twist of despairing anger towards Ralph. He knew how she felt about accepting gifts from him—he'd tricked her with this, swearing it was nothing more than a memento. How could he have done such a thoughtless thing! Furiously she jerked her wrist free and undid the bracelet's clasp with trembling fingers.

'Here,' she said bitterly. 'Take it. I have no idea whatsoever of its value, and frankly I care not at all. The only vaue it's ever held for me is a sentimental one—because it was given to me by someone I care about. Had I known of its monetary value, I'd never have accepted it.'

Amber eyes glittered sardonically back at her as he took the bracelet from her nerveless fingers.

'A touching little gesture,' he said evenly. 'I suppose you expect me to respond by insisting you keep my brother's gift. However, I believe it belongs with someone considerably more deserving.'

'And that person is very welcome to it,' Tessa hissed back through gritted teeth. 'Now look, I can promise you that when Ralph finds out about all of this, he'll be only too glad to put you straight on a few things since you're clearly not prepared to listen to a word I say. So if you'd be kind enough to tell him I've been here, I'd be most grateful. I shall book into a hotel somewhere and telephone him from there.'

'Why do you want to see him?'

'Why?' A dozen heated answers sprang to her lips, but she bit them back resolutely. 'Well, for one thing I'd like to pass on my very sincere congratulations in person,' she managed to grit out at last.

He shook his head decisively. 'No, Miss Edwards, I can't pass on your message to Ralph. And frankly I wouldn't, even if I could.'

'But why?'

'Because I have no intention of allowing you to screw things up between him and Janine.'

'That's ridiculous!' She could feel the heat of pure blazing anger flood her cheeks. How dared he say such a thing! 'I would never. . .'

'No, you wouldn't, because you're not going to get the chance.' Marc ran his eyes blatantly over her body and she shuddered, raked by the contempt in his gaze.

'Ralph is a good man, but inclined to be weak-willed. Janine is a fine girl, even if she doesn't possess your more obvious attractions. For once in his life he appears set to do the right and sensible thing. I don't want him to be deflected.'

'Even if I could deflect him, as you put it, why on earth would I want to?' It took everything she possessed to make her voice sound calm and reasonable, a million miles removed from the way she was actually feeling.

'Because you're clearly afraid the honey-pot he's provided for you will dry up once he's married.' Marc returned coldly. 'I believe you've come here in a bid to get him back.'

Tessa closed her eyes briefly, seriously beginning to wonder if she was losing her mind. This was a bad dream — it had to be. Any moment now she'd wake up and find herself at home, tucked up in a warm bed. Then a new thought struck her and she opened her eyes, glaring at him suspiciously.

'You said you couldn't pass on my message to Ralph. Why not?'

'Because I don't know where he is.' A fleeting glimmer of something approaching concern crossed his features, then he shrugged. 'He's disappeared.'

'Disappeared?' Her voice rose an octave on the single word. 'What on earth do you mean?'

He was clearly irritated by the question.

'Exactly what I said,' he returned shortly. 'He's gone. Vanished. Into thin air. Is that clear enough for you?'

'But he can't have! It was Ralph who asked me. . .' Suddenly realising what she was on the verge of blurting out, she stopped abruptly, biting her lip in dismay at her own thoughtlessness.

'It was Ralph who asked you to come here?' Marc eyed her narrowly as he completed the sentence for her. 'Well, that's very interesting, Miss Edwards. Very interesting indeed.' He fingered his square-cut jaw thoughtfully. 'Then perhaps you're just the lure I need to draw him out of hiding.'

'What makes you think he's gone into hiding?' She tried to inject scorn into her voice. 'He's a grown man. He may have simply gone to visit friends. Surely he doesn't have to answer to you for all of his movements. Or does he?'

His features tautened in dark annoyance and she berated herself silently for the taunt. Marc Duval wasn't the sort of man anyone in their right mind would readily annoy—but really, he was driving her crazy!

'No,' he answered at last. 'He doesn't have to answer to me. But I would have expected him to let Janine know where he was going.'

'And he hasn't?'

'No.'

'Then something could have happened to him! He might have been kidnapped.' Fear for Ralph showed clearly in her wide-set aquamarine eyes and strangely it seemed to annoy him all the more.

'I hardly think a kidnapper would have allowed him to pack a case full of clothes before snatching him,' he said caustically. 'In any case. . .' his lips thinned to a white line in his tanned face '. . .no one would be foolish enough to hold a member of my family to ransom.'

She heard the threat in his grim words and shuddered. 'How long has he been missing?'

'Just over a week.'

'A week!' She raised her hands in a helpless little gesture. 'He could be anywhere by now.'

'No. Not anywhere.' Marc shook his dark head decisively. 'He's still on the island.'

'How can you be so positive?' She eyed him curiously.

'Let's just say I have a lot of friends on Jersey.' He smiled coolly. 'They'd have let me know if he'd left.'

'They why on earth haven't you used those "friends" to track him down?'

Marc was silent for a long weighty moment. 'I don't want him to feel he's being brought to heel like a recalcitrant young pup,' he said at last, almost seeming to be speaking to himself more than to her. 'Though heaven knows, that is the way he behaves at times.' He glanced up, his amber eyes challenging her to comment. When she said nothing, he gave a faint shrug. 'I'd rather he decided to come back of his own free will.'

She was momentarily lost for words, thrown completely off balance by this completely unexpected glimpse of sensitivity in the elder Duval's soul. Given what she'd seen of him so far, she'd have expected him to go charging after Ralph, only too ready to whip him back into line, with no concern as to his younger brother's feelings in the matter.

'Why is it so important that he comes back?' she asked, a touch breathlessly. 'I mean—obviously he must come back eventually, for Janine's sake apart from anything else. But couldn't you simply leave him to return in his own time?'

Marc's expression grew grim. 'Everyone has to grow up eventually,' he said. 'Even my brother. He can't go on playing the part of the charming Peter Pan all his life. He has responsibilities—to himself and to me as well as to Janine.'

'You can't force him to accept those responsibilities,' she pointed out quietly.

'I don't intend to. I'm hoping that despite all evidence to the contrary, he has enough backbone to accept them for himself.'

'So what are you going to do?'

'Do?' His amber eyes gleamed strangely. 'I'm going to set a sprat to catch a mackerel, Miss Edwards. That's what I'm going to do.'

She frowned, mystified. 'I don't understand.'

'You claim to be my brother's closest friend. You also claim you're here at his invitation. So we'll have to make sure he gets to know you *are* here. That should bring him home.'

'And just how do you intend to do that?'

A mocking smile barely touched his lips. 'By monopolising your company for the next few days. By taking you all over the island and making sure you're seen. The jungle drums are very efficient on Jersey, Miss Edwards. Ralph will soon get the message, I'm quite sure.'

'That's the most ridiculous idea I've ever heard in my life!' If she'd been surprised by his apparent sensitivity a few short moments ago, this new twist completely overturned that. This cavalier assumption that he could simply make use of her for his own ends, coupled with being described as a sprat, made her bristle indignantly. But she also detected an element of fear in her hostility—fear of spending time in his company. And it wouldn't take a genius to work out the cause of that fear, she realised with a twist of anguish. She was afraid of Marc Duval—or, more accurately, she was afraid of the way he made her feel. To feel such immediate longing for someone was a totally new experience in her life—but to feel it for Ralph's brother was nothing sort of devastating. In a strange way, the very fact of acknowledging that physical attraction was an act of disloyalty to Ralph—their relationship had never been anything other than platonic, but she knew the deep-seated sense of inferiority he felt where his brother was concerned. For Tessa to be so drawn to Marc was in itself a betrayal. She couldn't do that to him—but after those heated moments of passion in Marc's arms she had no faith in her own strength to resist him. Steeling herself, she glared up at him. 'You'll have to find him yourself. I won't be dragged into this. I'm leaving right away.'

'Suit yourself.'

Anticipating battle, she'd already opened her mouth to give him another blast of invective, but now she closed it, thoroughly confused.

'Suit myself?'

He nodded. 'You can walk out of that door right now if you want to.' His mouth narrowed threateningly. 'But you won't get very far.'

'Are you threatening me?'

His expression didn't alter. 'A threat—a promise—call it what you will.'

Her knees seemed to sag beneath her and she was

forced to grab the windowsill for support as the world tipped temporarily off its axis.

'You look rather pale, Miss Edwards.' His solicitous tone was shot through with contempt. 'Perhaps you'd like to go upstairs to one of our guest bedrooms. Come — I'll show you the way.'

He took her arm and she started violently away, stunned by the jolt his very touch gave her.

'Don't touch me,' she hissed. 'Lay a single finger on me and I swear I'll make you regret it if it's the last thing I ever do.'

'Really?' He seemed amused by the threat. 'Strange words from a woman who was responding passionately in my arms just a few short moments ago.'

She'd never hated anyone in her life, but in that moment she was gripped by loathing, dark and corrosive. She wanted to lash out at him, to feel the physical satisfaction of landing a punch on his granite jaw. As the longing grew to all but overwhelming, she clenched her hands into fists at her sides but held her arms rigid, refusing to give in to the impulse. She had to get herself out of this — but she certainly wasn't going to do it through physical force. One glance at that powerfully built body was enough to tell her that. He could overpower her in seconds. No. This called for subtlety. The realisation made her sigh inwardly — since she was generally frank and straightforward, she wasn't exactly adept in the art of being devious. But she'd have to learn. And fast.

'Very well, Mr Duval.' She gave him her best shot at a convincingly resigned look. 'I see I have little choice. I'll accept your terribly kind offer of accommodation.'

A strange look flitted over his features, but after a heavily silent moment he gave a single nod.

'Good. Then come with me. I'll take you to your room.'

It was a beautiful room, light and airy and dominated by a huge old-fashioned bed, its brass fittings gleaming brightly. Under different circumstances she'd have been delighted to stay here. As it was, no matter how comfortable the room, it was nevertheless still a prison. But it wasn't Alcatraz. There must be a way to escape from it.

'Jeanne will be serving dinner in an hour,' Marc informed her.

'Well, I hope dinner isn't a terribly formal occasion here, since I didn't bring my best tiara with me.' Tessa bit down on her bottom lip as irritation glittered in his amber eyes. There she went again, letting her mouth run away with her before she'd fully engaged her brain as her oldest brother would say. But he drove her to it.

He crossed the room in a couple of long-legged strides and threw open the doors of the wardrobe.

'You can borrow something from in here,' he said curtly.

Intrigued, Tessa eyed the packed rail of clothes.

'You keep a special wardrobe for your prisoners?' she said incredulously. 'I hadn't realised you made a habit out of holding people against their will.'

His mouth became an angry white line.

'I'd advise you not to antagonise me, Miss Edwards,' he said in a voice that was soft, yet laden with threat. 'At the moment I'm prepared to endeavour to make your stay a pleasant one. Don't give me any reason to do otherwise.'

As he turned on his heel and strode from the room she felt a shiver run over her skin. How could two brothers possibly be so different? Ralph was like a playful breeze, light-hearted and charmingly irresponsible. Marc was like a mountain, awesome and immovable.

Of course life had dealt the two brothers very different hands of cards, she acknowledged, striving to be fair. Marc had still been in his teens when his parents died, leaving him with not only the burden of the family business, but also the upbringing of a small and doubtless bewildered brother. That he'd chosen to shoulder the burden spoke volumes for his strength of character. But it didn't excuse him being an arrogant, high-handed grouch. And it made it all the more galling that she should find herself attracted to him in a way she never had been to Ralph. But above all it didn't give him the right to treat her in this way.

Galvanised by the thought, she crossed to the open window and looked out, her eyes narrowing as she weighed up the prospects for escape. Then she gave a little whoop of delight as she spotted trelliswork bearing some sort of creeper plant, starting just a couple of feet below the sill and stretching almost to ground level.

'So, Mr Marc Duval,' she murmured with soft triumph, 'you may think you have the bird caged, but she's going to fly. Just you watch her!'

She turned away from the window, humming quietly to herself. There was no point trying to get away now — with her current run of luck, she'd probably run straight into a gardener, or the housekeeper Jeanne. She'd wait till the household had gone to bed, then at least she'd be assured of a head start. By the time her absence was discovered she could be at the airport, and surely even Marc wouldn't attempt to stop her getting on a plane.

Then she groaned, suddenly remembering Ralph's letter. How could she leave the island without at least trying to give him the help he'd asked for? But what sort of help could it possibly be? And why had he disappeared? Puzzled anew, she pulled his letter from her pocket and gazed at it, desperately trying to read between the lines. Then her attention was caught by the postmark. It had been posted from the island more than a fortnight ago — while she was still exploring a stretch of Tasmanian wilderness, camera in hand. It must have been lying in her home for days, she realised for the first time. He must have thought she was ignoring his appeal, since she hadn't immediately responded. Could that be why he'd vanished?

Glancing at the watch on her slender wrist, she grimaced. The master of the house had said dinner would be served in an hour — heaven forfend that she should risk his displeasure by being late! She returned to the wardrobe, her expression pessimistic as she wondered just what sort of ragbag selection it would have to offer. But it was with a growing sense of wonder that she rifled through the hangers, astonished to find a collection of clothes that wouldn't have shamed a top designer, and furthermore they looked to be in her size.

She frowned darkly, annoyed by her own sense of pique as she wondered just who the clothes belonged to. Some fashion-conscious girlfriend of Marc's, no doubt. With his looks, not to mention his bank balance, he must be able to attract any woman he fancied. She could easily visualise him out on the town with some long-legged, full-breasted beauty on his arm, the toast of Jersey society. The very notion made her stomach muscles clench painfully, and she reached into the wardrobe, fully intending to grab the first thing that came to hand, only to find a most uncharacteristic streak of vanity coming to the fore. After tonight, if the gods were kind, she'd never have to set eyes on Marc Duval again—for reasons she didn't want to explore too deeply, she wanted his last image of her to be a memorable one.

'Eureka!' She lifted a hanger from the rail and inspected the dress carefully. In deliciously slithery, silky material it was a wrap-over affair of gold and black—the sort of dress only a tall, willowy and preferably blonde woman could wear with panache. It could have been tailor-made for her. Unfortunately the wardrobe didn't possess a single pair of shoes in her size—she was childishly delighted to discover the owner of the clothes had considerably bigger feet than her own—and her rucksack contained only flipflops. Of course she could wear her walking boots and a pair of thick socks, but something told her Marc wouldn't see the funny side of that. So she'd just have to go barefoot. And barefaced too, since she had no make-up, but that caused her little grief. She rarely used cosmetics, disliking the feel of anything more than a light coating of moisturiser on her skin.

A short while later she turned curiously to the full-length mirror and blinked in surprise, quite taken aback by her own image. Since she lived most of her life in jeans or safari gear, the woman gazing back at her was a revelation. Even without make-up, she looked poised, sophisticated, the draping material moulding to her figure, emphasising the soft swell of her breasts, the curve of her waist, the gentle flare of her hips. She'd never looked so—so *womanly*! Ralph would never recognise her like this—she could barely recognise herself.

A faintly mysterious smile playing about her soft mouth, she made her way downstairs, her bare feet making no sound on the thickly piled carpet. Hearing the sounds of Marc's voice coming from the library, she headed in that direction, pausing in the open doorway as she realised he was talking on the telephone. She was about to back out again when he turned towards her and she was rooted to the spot, mesmerised by the sight of him in a dark, exquisitely cut suit, set off perfectly by a snowy white shirt and deep red tie. He was gorgeous, she thought despairingly—utterly, awesomely, drop-dead gorgeous, and every female cell in her body was tinglingly aware of it.

His amber eyes raked over her in sardonic appraisal, his lips quirking slightly as he spotted her shoeless state, but registering no other emotion.

'The answer's no,' he said decisively into the telephone mouthpiece. 'I've outlined my terms, and I'm not prepared to change them. Take them or leave them, but make up your mind fast. I won't waste time on this deal.'

He laid the receiver down and she almost felt sorry for the poor soul at the other end of the line. If he was attempting to haggle over something, he was clearly on to a loser. Marc Duval wasn't the sort of man to offer compromise or concession.

'Drink?'

His curt, clipped enquiry cut into her reverie and she nodded automatically.

'White wine, please. If you have it.'

He poured wine into two long-stemmed glasses and held one out towards her. But as she walked across the room to take it, she stepped on something sharp and fell to her knees with a yelp, her features contorted in pain.

'What is it? Let me see.' It was a command rather than a request, and she cupped her aching foot in both hands, shielding it from his view.

'It's nothing. I stepped on something sharp, that's all.'

'It's a piece of bone.' He picked up the offending object, then tossed it into a nearby wastepaper basket. Seeing her puzzled look, he smiled grimly. 'Mistral must have brought his supper in here.'

'Mistral?'

'My dog. Now let me look at your foot.' He knelt beside her and with a gentleness that surprised her, took her foot in his hands. His thumbs were warm as they pressed carefully into her skin and she drew her breath in sharply.

'Did that hurt?' His amber eyes searched her face and she shook her head. It wasn't pain that had made her flinch, but the incredible sensations sent flooding through her body by the touch of his fingers. She'd never really believed feet could be an erogenous zone. Until now. There could be no other way to interpret the heat rippling over her skin as anything other than purely sensual. It could only be because no one had ever touched her feet before, she told herself firmly. They were unexplored territory and all the more sensitive because of it.

'You're going to have a bruise there,' Marc said. 'It'll be tender to walk on.'

'I'll be fine.' She was dismayed to hear a breathless huskiness in her own voice. Anyone would think she was an impressionable teenager swooning over her favourite rock star, she thought disparagingly. She was normally famed for her ability to stay cool under pressure—so where had that disappeared to, just when she needed it most! 'If you'll just let me get up, I'll. . .'

'Put your arms round my neck.'

'What!' She sat bolt upright, her eyes widening to their fullest extent.

His features tautened impatiently. 'You heard,' he said curtly. 'Put your arms round my neck. I'll carry you to a chair.'

'There's really no need. I can walk perfectly well on my own.' She'd intended the rebuff to be starchily offputting, but his very nearness was making her flustered, his warm and unmistakably masculine scent assailing her senses, making her head swim.

'Do as you're told,' he shot back brusquely. Balancing on one knee, he slid an arm beneath her legs and bent his head towards her, apparently expecting docile obedience. For a moment she glowered at him, then with a sigh gave in, realising he wasn't about to back down. But as he pulled her against his body, the sudden surge of adrenalin sent coursing through her by his very nearness completely panicked her and she made one wild lunge to free herself. The move pulled him off balance just as he was rising, and she found herself spreadeagled on the floor beneath him.

'You stupid little. . .' His eyes shot amber sparks as he glared furiously down into her face. 'What on earth did you do that for?'

Any possibility of an acid retort was completely lost to her, not only because the tumble had knocked the breath out of her, but because having him lying on top of her had robbed her of the power of speech. Her every nerve-ending seemed to be throbbing in chorus; she was awash with a myriad sensations, devastating in their intensity. Unconsciously she licked her dry lips and his eyes were drawn to the tiny, telling gesture. His features darkened menacingly.

'My God, that was no accident, was it? So that's your game—you've set your snares out for me now that Ralph's no longer available.' Even as she tried to shake her head in angry denial, his lips twisted scornfully. 'Then you'd better learn that, unlike my brother, I'm far from easy prey. In fact, my pretty little predator, this is one occasion when the huntress has met her match.'

# CHAPTER FOUR

TESSA wanted to scream at Marc, wanted to pierce his seemingly impenetrable skin with verbal daggers as sharp as the ones he'd used to flay her. But most of all she wanted him to close the tiny gap left between them and brand her hungry mouth with searing kisses. He had set something on fire within her, a spark threatening to rage into conflagration, and she had no means of fighting back. She gazed up at him now, her eyes cloudy and dazed as she did internal battle with herself, desperately searching for some hidden reserve of strength.

'You've got me all wrong,' she managed at last, but her voice was barely more than a whisper.

'Really?' There was a wealth of scorn in the single scathing word. 'So if I were to give you the choice right now between Ralph and me, just how would you choose, Tessa Edwards?'

Caught in the thrall of something too powerful even to name, Tessa tried to look away from his penetrating gaze, feeling the sting of tears in her eyes as her lashes fluttered downwards. How could he even ask her to choose? she wondered helplessly — Ralph had been her best friend for years, yet theirs had been a relationship based on fondness and affection, with no physical element whatsoever. She'd met Marc only a few short hours ago, and they'd done nothing but argue, yet here in his arms she knew a strange and totally incomprehensible feeling of rightness. If he were to kiss her now, she'd melt clean away in his arms.

'I'm here only because you're forcing me to be,' she managed to grit out at last.

He laughed but there was no amusement in the harsh sound. 'Yet your body seems to be in no rush to get away,' he said. He lifted himself away from her fractionally and she glanced down, following the direction of his eyes, only to feel a rush of embarrassed warmth flood her cheeks as she saw the hard buds of her nipples pressing against the thin material of the flamboyant black and gold dress. 'Your body wants to be touched,' he said softly, and she was incapable of moving as his hand slid along her arm. The tiny part of her brain still functioning deeply resented the way he was making her feel, but its lone mutinous voice was drowned out by the clamour of a million other voices, insistently begging for more.

'It's nothing but a physical attraction,' she groaned, the breath catching in her throat as his hand finally touched one aching breast, his fingers lightly stroking her sensitised skin through the silky dress. 'It means nothing.'

'So anyone could make you feel this way?' Slowly, tantalisingly, he dipped his head and she shuddered with the warmth of his breath on her skin. She was lost for an answer, her normally quicksilver wits befuddled and dazed by sheer longing. If she said yes, she'd sound promiscuous and that was a million miles removed from the truth. If she said no, it would be tantamount to telling him how much she wanted him — and only him — and she had way too much pride for that. As she searched her fragmented consciousness for an answer, he pushed aside the flimsy barrier of silk and touched her naked breasts, tracing a blazing path with his hands and with his mouth, sparking a wild strangeness in her soul, an elemental need that was stronger and more powerful than anything she'd ever experienced. Unknowing, unaware of what she was doing, she arched up against him and groaned deep in her throat with the feel of his answering need, hard against her.

'Tell me.' He raised his head from her breasts to look into her eyes, his own expression dark and unreadable. 'Tell me what you want, Tessa.'

The words strangled in her throat—words that would have told him she'd gone far beyond want—far beyond anything that still allowed her the luxury of choice. Now there was only need, sheer, overwhelming need—and shamingly it was a need that existed only for him. No other hands could ever touch her as he was touching her now, no other mouth could ever bring her to the brink of such trembling ecstasy, no other eyes could look so deeply into her own that they must surely see straight through to her soul. And no one else could ever burn themselves into her psyche as he was doing now.

It was that final realisation that gave her the strength, born of desperation, to turn her head away from his kiss. The tiny move took everything she had, every shred of willpower, and left only loss where there should have been triumph.

'This is crazy,' she murmured brokenly. 'I don't even know you.'

'Does that matter?' It was scant consolation that the words seemed torn from him.

'It does to me.'

'Or are you simply afraid I'll tell Ralph?' His lips twisted savagely, lips which only seconds before had been both promising and delivering sensuous delights. With an angry exclamation he pushed himself away from her and she lay still for a second, still dazed by the onslaught of all she'd been feeling. 'That's closer to the truth, isn't it, Tessa? You're still harbouring hopes of snaring my brother—probably because he's considerably more malleable than me. Much easier to manipulate.'

She shook her head, her spirit slowly beginning to return to life.

'You're wrong.'

'No, Tessa Edwards—it's you who are wrong. Wrong to believe I would ever allow Ralph to fall into your money-grabbing little hands.' His eyes grew cold as ice as they swept contemptuously over her dishevelled state. 'Now I suggest you make yourself respectable. Jeanne will be waiting to serve dinner. I don't want to waste any more of her time.'

She escaped to her room as soon after dinner as pride would allow. It had been a miserable meal, served and eaten mostly in silence. Distantly she'd recognised a skilful hand behind the cooking, and since she was normally blessed with a healthy appetite she felt a faint sense of regret in being unable to do justice to the succulent seafood selection which, Marc coldly informed her, was an island speciality. It could have been five-star cuisine for all she knew. Every mouthful had turned to dust as soon as it reached her mouth, and it was only with the greatest of difficulty that she was able to swallow any of it.

But she'd kept her spine ramrod-straight, refusing to give him the satisfaction of knowing how she was really feeling. She'd even managed to smile and thank Jeanne for the delicious spread, which only went to prove she was a much better actress than she'd given herself credit for, she thought ironically as she stepped out of the dress and returned it to its hanger.

Dressed only in a skimpy pair of briefs, she cast a look of rueful longing at the bed. It was a particularly nice bed — deep and inviting and promising rest and comfort for the most tired and jaded soul. Right now she couldn't remember ever feeling more tired or jaded in all her twenty-five years. Even in a life that was rarely restful and never boring, the last few days had been memorable. No, strike that, she thought forcefully — as soon as she managed to get away from here, she was going to forget this period of undiluted trauma as swiftly as possible. But that still left the problem of Ralph — and his cry for help — unresolved.

With a heavy sigh she subsided on to the edge of the bed. She'd never turned away from a friend in need, even if the only thing she could offer was comfort or a shoulder to cry on. And even now she still felt indebted to Ralph for the comfort he'd given so generously when she'd been sorrowing over Dan. To think of running out on him now went right against the grain. But what else could she do? If she stayed here in the Duval home she'd have to suffer the agonies of being close to Marc, and if she felt this churned up after just a few hours in his company, heaven help her after a few days!

No. She simply had to get away. There was no other alternative. Ralph would understand. Eventually.

Her decision made, and the lure of the big comfortable bed proving too much, Tessa swung her long legs up on to the mattress and pulled the top coverlet over her. On the bedside table she spotted a book on Jersey, presumably placed there for the benefit of guests, and picked it up with a rueful smile. Since she obviously wasn't going to get a chance to see much more of the island than she'd already viewed on the way from the airport, she might as well find out what she'd be missing. As tired as she was, the book proved engrossing — and tantalising — with its descriptions of spectacular bays and secluded inlets, and its snippets of information about Jersey's rich store of myths and legends, many of them associated with the sea. She was halfway through the tale of *La Loup Garou* — the Werewolf claimed to still haunt the Wolf's Caves on the north side of the island, when sleep finally overtook her and she plunged helplessly into a trying, turbulent dream. Unsurprisingly, the dream strongly featured Marc Duval — not as a werewolf, but in the shape of a black panther, even more terrifying as he stalked her as his prey. In her sleep she moved restlessly, a light sheen of perspiration breaking out on her forehead as she tried desperately to get away from the gleaming amber eyes.

Frankly it was a relief to wake up, though her eyes were puzzled on opening to an unfamiliar room. Then memory returned and she groaned heavily, remembering what lay ahead — and all that had just passed. A swift glance towards the window showed the pale light of dawn beginning to streak the sky. She didn't have any time to lose.

It took only moments to dress in shorts and a clean shirt from the rucksack Marc must have had sent up to her room the previous night. She gazed at the bulky pack for a moment, wondering how on earth she was going to shin down the trelliswork with that on her back, then gave a fatalistic shrug. She wasn't about to leave her things here with no guarantee of ever seeing them again, so she'd just have to manage somehow. She'd also have to make the descent barefoot, she realised, since her walking boots were too big and unwieldy to fit between the spaces of the trellis.

Stepping quietly over to the window, she held her breath as she slid the glass upwards, wincing as the wooden frame scraped jarringly. Never mind the window, she thought despairingly, her heart was beating loudly enough to alarm the entire neighbourhood. She maneouvred herself on to the sill and slid carefully down, her bare feet searching for toeholds in the lavish greenery. Then she gave an anguished yelp, swiftly smothered, as her already tender foot was mercilessly stabbed by thorns. Her legs were going to look like a relief map after this little escapade.

She was just a few feet from the ground when she was suddenly frozen to the spot by the sounds of low but determined growling. Apprehensively she glanced down and sucked her breath in sharply at the sight of a large and lethal-looking dog, its lips drawn back over teeth quite capable of ripping a grown man to shreds.

'Mistral,' she muttered in a hollow voice. Marc had mentioned the dog last night—she'd even stepped on his bone in the library. Why on earth hadn't it occurred to her that his pet might actually be a fully fledged guard dog? She wasn't afraid of dogs—under different circumstances she could probably have coaxed even this canine Colossus into eating out of her hand. But he was clearly on duty, and not taking too kindly to the sight of a human crawling down the side of the house.

'Well, this is a fine mess you've gotten yourself into,' she groaned, feeling the palms of her hands grow damp with fearful sweat. She was stuck, well and truly stuck. She'd managed to climb down with the cumbersome rucksack on her back, but climbing back up again would be well nigh impossible. And she couldn't spare two hands to undo all the straps and catches holding the backpack in place. Faced with those powerful jaws she clearly couldn't risk going down either. So she was stranded. And, given the early hour, she was likely to stay that way for some time.

At least the view was pleasant, she thought with a rueful stab at humour. The Duval home sat on top of a cliff, and if she craned her neck just a little she could see a tiny, inviting-looking bay far below. That must be where Ralph had played his childhood games, she mused, wishing she was down there right now, clambering over the rocks and walking barefoot on the sand instead of clinging to this wall like a complete fool. Her only remaining hope was that it was someone other than Marc who discovered her there.

That hope died some time later when she spotted his tall, unmistakable figure strolling round the side of the house.

'Well, well.' The dog's expression promptly switched from a snarl to a smile as Marc stopped at his side and absently stroked his head. 'What do we have here? A spot of early-morning mountaineering?'

'Very funny.' After being stuck for goodness knew how long, she was cramped and chilled and feeling the ache of countless thorn scratches. 'Would you be kind enough to inform this slavering beast that I'm not his breakfast?'

Marc shrugged his powerful shoulders indifferently. 'Come down and tell him yourself.'

Tessa eyed the animal warily and moved one foot experimentally, only to see its benign expression turn instantly threatening.

'What's wrong, Tessa?' Marc's voice was even, yet there was no mistaking the underlying taunt. 'You're not scared, are you?' Before she could summon up a suitably scathing response, he moved to the bottom of the wall. 'Come on, slither down. I'll catch you.'

Frankly in that moment she wasn't sure which she feared more, Marc's arms or the dog's jaws, but she didn't exactly have a lot of choice. With a pained sigh she forced her stiff body to move, feeling ever more ridiculous and ever more resentful that she should have landed in such a humiliating position in the first place. When she finally touched down on terra firma she had to force her eyes upward to meet his, sure she'd read only scorn and contempt there. Instead she could have sworn there was a faint glint of amusement lurking in the amber depths, but told herself not to be so foolish. He hadn't struck her as a man of great humour, thus far at least.

To her relief he made no comment, but simply watched as she shrugged the rucksack from her aching back, wincing as she flexed her tired and cramped shoulders.

'Feeling a little stiff?'

She glared at him, covering her embarrassment with indignation.

'Of course I'm stiff,' she shot back hotly. 'I've been

stuck on that blasted wall for hours. And don't you dare tell me it was all my own fault—what else was I supposed to do when I'm little better than a prisoner here?'

'I wasn't about to say any such thing,' he returned equably, cutting her tirade short. 'I'd probably have done the same thing myself.' Strong white teeth flashed in an unexpected wry smile that creased his eyes at the corners and slammed into her like a hammer blow. How could a smile possibly be so devastating? She thought dazedly, suddenly finding the simple act of breathing to be beyond her. It could only be because of its rarity. 'However, I might have thought to arm myself with a succulent decoy for the dog,' he continued. 'Particularly since I told you in the library last night that I had one.'

A sudden memory of all that had happened in the library last night sent a red flush to her cheeks and she looked away, unable to meet his knowing eyes.

'Speaking of which. . .'

She tensed, wondering what on earth he was about to say. Surely even he couldn't be cruel enough to taunt her further about her behaviour in his arms? Behaviour which seemed even worse when looked at in the cool light of day.

'Yes?'

'It looks as if you've added a few new bruises with your little climbing adventure.' His eyes ran over her assessingly and she suffered his scrutiny in pained silence. 'You'd better come into the house and get those scratches seen to.'

She was taken aback by his unexpected concern. 'That's really not necessary,' she said with stiff dignity.

'Then stay here.' Impatience sliced into his tones. 'I'll leave Mistral on guard till you come to your senses.'

Tessa glanced sideways at the dog and scowled darkly. 'Oh, all right!' With bad grace she stalked off towards the front door, Marc following with the dog padding happily at his heels.

'We'll go to my office,' he said. 'There's a first-aid kit in there.'

'This is your office?' She stopped dead on the threshold, her aquamarine eyes wide with astonishment. 'You could run the United States from in here!' Awed by the collection of computer hardware, she glanced about her. 'What on earth do you need all of this for?'

He shrugged off-handedly as he opened the first-aid case on the wall and selected several items. 'I keep my main base here on Jersey, but I have business interests all over the world. I need to keep in touch with them all. And with the stock market, of course. Sit down there.'

Unthinkingly she obeyed, too fascinated by everything she was seeing to cavil at his command. But when he knelt before her, she gazed at him in clear astonishment.

'I can manage perfectly well. . .' Her words disappeared in a yelp as he lifted one foot into his lap. 'Really, Marc, there's no need. . .' She flinched as he dabbed antiseptic fluid on to one of the worst scratches on her leg, though in truth she wasn't sure if she was reacting to the stinging pain or the tingling rush of blood caused by the touch of his warm fingers on her cool bare skin. He ignored her protest and carried on with his ministrations. Mesmerised by the sight of his dark head bent over her leg, she knew a longing to push her fingers into his thick luxuriant hair, to lift his head, to press her mouth to the stark planes of his face, and finally to taste his lips with her own. Horrified by her own wayward thoughts, she tore her eyes away and glanced round the room.

'So this is how modern-day pirates operate,' she mused aloud. 'Ouch!'

'That's a particularly deep scratch,' he said. 'You'll probably need a covering on it. What was that about pirates?' His tone was deceptively mild, but she wasn't fooled.

'Just a throwaway comment,' she returned. 'Surely you don't object? Weren't some of your ancestors pirates? Or is that just local legend?'

He shook his head. 'No. That's a historical fact. But those were desperate times. People did what they had to in order to survive.'

'You seem to be surviving pretty well.' It was a glib comment and she regretted it as soon as she saw the dark tightening of his features. 'I mean. . .'

'I know exactly what you mean,' he shot back acidly. 'You've been looking around you and mentally calculating just how much I must be worth. Perhaps even working out the best way to get your sticky little fingers on the Duval wealth.' His amber eyes bored into her and she was hard pressed not to shudder beneath the contempt in his gaze. 'So tell me, Miss Tessa Edwards — doesn't that make you a pirate too?'

Tessa bit down hard on her bottom lip, refusing to let herself yell back at him, as much as she wanted to. Yet one part of her regretted the return to antagonism, particularly since she'd sparked it off herself. For just a few minutes as he'd tended to her scratches, there had been a truce, and it had been a welcome one. But it seemed they were forever destined to be at one another's throats, and maybe it was best that way. At least if they were arguing there was no danger of landing up in his arms again—frankly she didn't think she had the strength to resist another encounter of that kind. Her body was growing warm at the very idea, much to her dismay. Just what was it about this man that she could long for his touch even as she burned with indignation? It made no sense.

'What happens now?' she said in a low voice, refusing to respond to his pirate gibe.

'Exactly what I told you last night,' he said with quietly grim satisfaction. 'You and I are going to launch our campaign to find Ralph—or rather, to let him know you're here.' He smiled without humour. 'I'll take you on a guided tour of Jersey.'

## CHAPTER FIVE

'THIS is the zoo.'

Tessa slid Marc a sideways glance of marked astonishment. When he'd said he'd take her on a guided tour of the island, this was the last place she'd expected him to choose as their first port of call.

'I'm well aware of that,' he returned evenly. 'I have some business to do here, and I thought it would be a good place to start laying the bait, so to speak. Besides which...' he eyed her consideringly '...I thought you might enjoy seeing the place. Though of course seeing the animals might prove something of a busman's holiday to you.'

'On the contrary!' An irrepressible smile of delight curved her generous mouth. 'I've always wanted to visit Jersey Zoo—I've read a great deal about it and the work they do here.'

He seemed momentarily taken aback by her obvious pleasure, the characteristic grimness fading from his features. 'The zoo is famous worldwide,' he agreed.

'They're having a good day,' she commented as they passed through a car park filled to overflowing with cars and tour coaches.

He shrugged his broad shoulders and she found herself wondering absently if it was difficult to find clothes to fit a frame so powerful. The light grey sweatshirt and jeans he was wearing today fitted him like a second skin, clinging with loving delineation to his tautly muscled form.

'This is fairly normal,' he returned. 'During the summer, at least. In the winter things are quieter.'

She shot him a glance of wry amusement. 'You sound as though you're a regular visitor,' she said, not believing it for one moment. A zoo was hardly the sort of place Marc Duval would choose to frequent. He made no answer, but simply handed over the admission fee at the reception desk.

'Good morning, Marc,' the middle-aged attendant greeted him warmly. 'How nice to see you again.' She nodded amiably at Tessa. 'And nice to see you too, miss. Is he trying to convert you to the cause?'

Perplexed, Tessa could only manage a smile in return. But as they walked into the park itself, she turned to him with a frown.

'What did she mean? What cause?'

'Staff here at the zoo are passionate about the place and all it tries to do,' he returned. 'They work very hard to ensure their message gets across to everyone who visits.'

'Message?' Despite herself she was curious.

He nodded. 'That this isn't simply a place where people can come and gape at unusual exhibits. Its prime function is the preservation and breeding of endangered species.' He gave her a questioning look. 'I'd have expected a wildlife photographer to know that.'

The comment made her bridle. 'I do know that,' she returned stiffly. 'As I just said, I've always wanted to visit Jersey Zoo, and I'm a great admirer of their work. I'm just surprised that you seem to know so much.'

One jet-black eyebrow quirked sardonically. 'Because modern-day pirates don't normally take much interest in conservation? Ah—but despite all your preconceived notions, sweet Tessa, you don't know a great deal about me at all.'

'Well, that's rich coming from you, I must say!' She stopped dead in her tracks and whirled round to face him, completely oblivious to the interested looks of the other zoo visitors. 'Who are you to speak of preconceived notions, may I ask? Considering the way you've got me marked down as gold-digger, when you've got absolutely no evidence to back it up, I think that's a bit much, frankly!'

'No evidence?' His even tones were belied by the spark of anger in his leonine eyes. 'Except that by some strange coincidence you turned up on my doorstep just after a magazine article about my brother's wedding, claiming to be his dearest friend even though he's never even seen fit to mention your name in my presence. Not forgetting of course that you were blatantly sporting a Duval family heirloom on your wrist.' He shook his head wonderingly. 'Ralph may be foolish in many ways, but I'd never have expected him to just give away something of such strong sentimental value.'

'Then doesn't that tell you something about our friendship?'

His lips twisted savagely. 'Frankly, no. It simply tells me you must have had Ralph dangling on a string. But then he always was a sucker for big-eyed blondes.'

She turned away, too hurt even for anger. How could she ever hope to convince this cold-eyed, disbelieving man? As for the bracelet—Ralph could never have envisaged the trouble it would land her in when he'd given her the pretty, fragile little chain. It had been just after his graduation, she recalled now with a faint smile. Marc hadn't been able to make it over to the mainland for the ceremony, detained on the island by some last-minute emergency. Ralph had concealed his disappointment, but knowing him as well as she did, she knew how deeply he was hurt by his brother's absence, and she'd felt a stab of very real dislike for the man who could put business before family.

'It's better this way,' Ralph had announced cheerfully as she hugged him after he'd received his degree diploma. 'I'd never have made it to the graduation without you nagging and pushing me all the way.' He'd held her away to arm's length, his expression uncharacteristically serious. 'I mean it, you know, Tess,' he said solemnly. 'You've been a real rock for me — always there when I needed you. I could never have asked for a better, truer friend.'

Touched by his words, she'd reached up to plant a kiss on his cheek. 'That goes both ways,' she said softly. 'I'm sorry about Marc, though — I was looking forward to meeting your brother.'

'Maybe it's just as well he didn't come.' Ralph was grinning, but she could sense he wasn't speaking entirely in jest. 'Knowing his fatal attraction for the opposite sex, you'd probably have fallen head over heels for him — and I'm not sure I could have coped with that. This is *my* day, after all.'

They'd gone for a meal then, Tessa for once ditching her principles and allowing Ralph to take her to the flashiest and most expensive restaurant in the city in honour of the celebration. They'd drunk a little too much champagne, and grown as silly and giggly as two schoolchidren, though the unspoken awareness was ever present between them that this was the parting of the ways. At the end of the evening, he'd taken her hand in his, his eyes warm as he looked at her.

'I know you don't like accepting gifts, Tess,' he began, 'which makes you unique in my experience! But I want you to have something to remember me by none the less.'

'As if I could ever forget you, you big idiot,' she said teasingly. 'I don't need a souvenir to do that.'

'Maybe not,' he continued stubbornly, 'but I want you to have it anyway.' He placed something in her hand and closed her fingers over it before she could even look at it. 'It's nothing special, just a little trinket. But keep it anyway. Please.'

Something in his eyes blocked the protest forming at her lips and after a long moment she nodded.

'OK, Ralph,' she murmured. 'I will keep it. But don't think this lets you off the hook! I can still keep on nagging you — even from long-distance!'

Tessa rubbed her wrist absent-mindedly now, missing the bracelet's delicate caress on her skin. Blast Ralph and blast the bracelet, she thought with sudden savagery — but most of all blast Marc for his bloody-mindedness!

Looking up now she saw the contempt in his amber eyes and shivered even as she tilted her chin in open defiance. His scorn had cut her like a knife, even though she knew it to be unjustified. Yet why should that be? With anyone else she might have felt regret, perhaps even a faint sense of righteous anger at being so misunderstood, but she certainly wouldn't be suffering this deep inner ache. Why should it matter so much to her what Marc Duval thought?

'Look,' she said abruptly, giving up the struggle to understand, 'I'm sure we must have laid the bait now. Someone's bound to tell Ralph you've been here with me.'

He raised his eyebrows mockingly. 'Don't tell me you want to leave already?' he said. 'You've barely seen anything yet.'

She shook her head. 'No, I don't want to leave. But it's clearly no pleasure for either one of us to be stuck in the other's company. Why don't we split up and meet back at the café later?'

'And have you try another of your famous escapes?' He shot her a wry look. 'I don't think so. Now—which animal would you like to see first?'

Tessa clenched her hands into fists in an agony of frustration, but bit back the angry retort that sprang automatically to her tongue. Losing her temper did no good whatsoever—and since he always seemed to get the last word, it didn't even give her the satisfaction of catharsis. She returned his gaze, her blue eyes uncharacteristically stony.

'The golden-headed lion tamarins,' she said through gritted teeth, deliberately selecting one of the most obscure animals she could think of.

'A fine choice,' he returned with infuriating blandness. 'Follow me.'

And that was another shock. With unerring accuracy he led her straight to the tamarins, then at her bemused request to the snow leopards, Przewalski's horses, and the spectacled bears. All without benefit of even a guide book. To discover he was quite at home in the zoo was irritating in the extreme because it was so unexpected — but what made it still worse was the discovery that he was astonishingly knowledgeable about every animal they saw. And he didn't even display the remotest trace of conceit or smugness, she thought grouchily. Quite the contrary, in fact. The awful truth was, she couldn't have asked for a better companion.

So why should that annoy her? Shouldn't she be pleased to find herself, against all the odds, actually enjoying his company? It could only be that he'd upended all her expectations and she was finding that hard to come to terms with, she acknowledged with rueful frankness. But who would ever have expected Marc Duval, with his reputation as a shark and a pirate, to be just as passionately interested in conservation and wildlife as she was herself? Not only interested, but well-informed. The last straw came when she spotted his name on a plaque listing the zoo's main benefactors. Right at the top.

'Is there another Marc Duval on the island?' she asked unthinkingly.

He eyed her with mild curiosity. 'Not that I'm aware of. Why?'

She nodded towards the plaque. 'I'm simply surprised to see your name there,' she said, astonished to hear a snide note creeping into her voice, and hating the sound of it, but totally incapable of eradicating it. 'Philanthropy doesn't seem to go hand-in-hand with your type of business life. Unless of course it's a shrewd piece of PR on your part.'

He seemed more amused than annoyed. 'What's the matter, Tessa?' he asked quietly. 'Scared there won't be enough of the Duval cake left for you if I squander it on animals?'

'I wouldn't take any of the so-called Duval cake if it were handed to me on a plate!' she spat back furiously, cut to the quick by his barb, yet painfully aware she'd probably deserved it. 'It would choke me. When will you get it into your head that I do not, repeat not, want any of your blasted money! I'd rather rot in hell!'

He was unimpressed. 'That would be a terrible waste of a beautiful body, though the experience might just do your shrewish nature some good.' He turned on his heel and strode away then, leaving her spluttering in thwarted indignation. Damn and blast him! How could he and Ralph possibly be so very different? If she'd been here with Ralph, they'd have been laughing and joking together, enjoying the antics of the animals, instead of spitting at each other like wildcats.

She paused mid-thought, pursing her lips. Ralph would have made her laugh, it was true, but he wouldn't have had one fraction of the understanding of this place Marc possessed in bushels. He was unquestionably the most infuriating man she'd ever had the misfortune to encounter, but he was stimulating too — and challenging. He had a genuinely enquiring mind — when she'd casually mentioned one of her photographic safaris, he'd questioned her closely, clearly interested. That had been before they'd started arguing again — no, she corrected herself irritably — before *she'd* started arguing again. Why hadn't she been able to relax and simply enjoy his company?

Because she'd been afraid to, she admitted silently. Afraid she might discover she could like Marc Duval. Finding herself physically bowled over by him was bad enough, but if she were to thaw emotionally, she'd be completely sunk.

Feeling strangely disconsolate, she set off to follow him, only to stop in her tracks as she spotted him several feet away. He was talking to a woman, one he obviously knew well if his warm expression was anything to go by. Was she the owner of the clothes in the wardrobe? Was she the one who knew Marc well enough that she could keep an alternative set of clothes in his home? Then she shook her head, impatient with herself for even wondering. The woman was the wrong shape entirely—too small and way too voluptuous. She'd obviously like to have that sort of relationship with him, though—that much was clear from the way she was gazing up at him flirtatiously, her curvaceous body angled towards him invitingly. It wouldn't take a body language expert to decipher the message she was sending Marc, Tessa thought viciously, then blinked, taken aback by her own venom. She'd never been afflicted by the curse of jealousy in her life—even when she'd found Dan in another woman's arms, she hadn't been jealous as such, but simply hurt. But she was feeling it now all right, feeling the dagger plunged deep into her being twist deeper still with every flutter of the woman's eyelashes, every pout of her generous, glistening mouth. She wanted to turn away, despising herself for spying on them, yet found she was unable to move, rooted to the spot.

Marc was smiling down at the woman, his expression, even from a distance, clearly affectionate. It was the look he might give to a lover and light years removed from the way he looked at her, Tessa thought despairingly. Just for a fleeting moment she allowed herself to imagine she was in the woman's place, gazing up at him, feeling the warmth of his smile, and unconsciously her lips parted for the kiss that could surely be only seconds away.

It was at that very moment that Marc looked round and spotted her there and everything seemed to turn to ice within her as he smiled knowingly. Unconsciously she raised herself on to tiptoe, ready to turn and flee, but before she could make a move he called out to her.

'Tessa! Come and meet a friend of mine.'

On feet that seemed to be dragging weights of lead, she made her way over to them, barely aware of the other woman's look of displeasure.

'This is Tasha,' Marc said, and the woman gave a smile that came nowhere near her eyes. 'Tasha, this is Tessa—a friend of Ralph's.'

'Oh, really?' The woman visibly brightened, and gave Tessa an interested look. 'What brings you to Jersey?'

'She's come to see Ralph, of course,' Marc cut in before she could answer. 'To congratulate him and Janine in person. Unfortunately Ralph's taken himself off for a couple of days. . .' He made a lightly dismissive gesture with one hand. 'Probably afraid he'd be expected to do some of the organising.'

Tasha chuckled. 'That sounds like Ralph!' She leaned forward to pat Tessa on the hand. 'I'm sure he can't have gone very far.'

'If you should happen to bump into him, perhaps you could tell him you've seen Tessa,' Marc continued. 'It would be a shame if she had to return to the mainland without seeing him.'

'Of course I will. Now. . .' she sent Marc a coquettish look from beneath her lashes '. . .I really must run along. Why don't you give me a call some time? You know the number.'

As she sashayed away along the path, Marc turned to Tessa, amusement clear in his amber eyes.

'It's OK,' he said. 'She's gone. You can take that look off your face now.'

'What look?'

'The one that managed to smile even as it was sending daggers. If looks really could kill, poor Tasha would be lying stone dead at my feet right now.'

'I'm perfectly sure she'd have been happy to lie anywhere with you,' Tessa gritted out, then could happily have kicked herself. How could she had said something so blatantly revealing?

Marc nodded in slow satisfaction. 'What's the matter, Tessa? Scared she might get something you want?'

'I haven't the faintest idea what you mean.' She tossed her head contemptuously. 'The only thing she apparently wants is you. And she's very much more than welcome to you.'

She flinched as his fingers cupped round her cheek, gently but firmly bringing her round to face him. 'Are you so sure about that?' His words seemed to shiver over her skin, making her tremble. His thumb grazed over the fullness of her lower lip and he smiled mockingly as her pupils dilated, making her eyes seem larger than ever. 'You forget, sweet Tessa—I've already discovered the dichotomy in your soul.'

'Dichotomy?' The word stumbled from her lips as she fought to steady her breathing. 'What dichotomy?'

'The one which makes your body hunger for my touch even as your mind tries to reject me.'

'That's ridiculous and you know it!' She tried twist away from his hand to no avail.

'Do I? Then tell me what would happen right now if I were to give in to the pleading I see in those pretty eyes of yours, and kiss you?'

'Here?' She shot a horrified glance at the other visitors milling round the various animal enclosures. 'In front of all these people?'

He shrugged. 'Why not.'

'You wouldn't dare!'

'Wouldn't I?' He was openly challenging her now. 'Why don't you try me?'

Every remaining vestige of sense in her body screamed at her to back down while she still had the chance, but one renegade streak of obstinacy emerged above the rest, refusing to let her ignore the gauntlet he'd thrown down.

'Go ahead, then,' she said huskily. 'Kiss me. But if you think I'm going to fall apart the way your friend Tasha would doubtless do, you're very much mistaken.'

If the gibe had any effect, he gave no sign of it, simply leaning closer and closer with agonising slowness till she seemed to have lost the power to breathe altogether. When his lips touched hers, her eyes closed helplessly, her whole being becoming still, focused solely on the touch of his mouth.

Any embarrassment she might have felt at being kissed in so public a place evaporated instantly. She could have been on a deserted beach, or a lunar landscape, the only reality left to her the man who was moving his mouth over hers, the sensuality of his caress almost more than she could bear. He wasn't holding her, she could have pulled back any time she wanted to, but how could she pull away when every cell in her body wanted to move closer and closer still. His kiss was a revelation, tender and teasing, his teeth nibbling gently on her lower lip, his tongue darting playfully into her welcoming mouth. Longing for his touch, her breasts rubbed against the cotton of her shirt, her nipples puckering in silent demand for his attention, a core of heat building mercilessly deep within that must surely end in total meltdown.

It was Marc who finally broke away and she gazed up at him through clouded eyes, her breathing ragged and shallow.

'Let's get out of here,' he said urgently, and even as she tried to shake her head she found herself nodding instead. She was out of control, she realised desperately as she followed him to the car—he wanted to make love to her, and there was nothing she could do to still the fires raging mercilessly within her. It was all wrong—she didn't love him, and he certainly didn't love her, and underneath everything else lay a burning shame that she should even be contemplating sleeping with this man who was, apart from everything else, Ralph's brother.

She'd be nothing more than the latest in what was probably a long line of easy conquests, yet it seemed to count for nothing. For the first time in her life, her head was relinquishing control to her heart—no, not her heart, she corrected herself ruthlessly. This had nothing to do with her heart. It was simply that her inexperienced body had recognised the touch of a master and wanted more. Much, much more. She was silent in the car, gazing sightlessly through the window at a succession of farmhouses, all built in the granite that Ralph had once told her the island was renowned for—he'd found it delightful that the university city of Aberdeen also had a dominance of the same enduring stone, she remembered distractedly.

They drove on through narrow leafy lanes, past lush green fields filled with the distinctive and almost deer-like Jersey cattle, along narrow leafy lanes and past fields of flowers. Normally the tranquil beauties of the island would have entranced her, but today she barely saw them, too bewildered and disorientated by the turmoil within to fully absorb anything else.

At last though, realising they were on an unfamiliar road, she managed to drag herself out of the morass of her troubled feelings long enough to ask, 'Where are we going? This isn't the way back to the house.'

He slanted a smile in her direction. 'I was beginning to think you must have gone to sleep. You haven't said a word in ages. I'm taking you on a shopping trip to St Helier.'

If he'd said they were going on a voyage to the moon she couldn't have been more stunned. She'd been so convinced he was taking her home with every intention of taking her to bed—indeed, she'd spent the entire journey desperately trying to marshal the few tattered defences still left in her, in hopes that she'd be able to resist. To discover his real intentions was profoundly shocking.

'A shopping trip?' she echoed weakly. 'What for?'

There was a strange glint in his amber eyes as he glanced at her. 'Our affectionate little display at the zoo, coupled with Tasha's legendary appetite for gossip should have worked wonders,' he said evenly. 'The news will probably be halfway round the island by now. I'm going to take you out to dinner tonight, and that will doubtless ensure even more coverage.' A mocking smile touched his mouth. 'However, I think most of our restaurants would look somewhat askance at you turning up barefoot, so we'd better find some suitable footwear.'

His words, so cool and devoid of emotion, thudded into her like an ungloved fist, and it took everything she possessed not to show the pain he'd inflicted so casually.

'Is that what the "affectionate little display" was all about?' she managed to grit out, her voice low but tightly controlled. 'A sideshow for Ralph's benefit?'

He shrugged. 'What else?'

She slumped back against the cool leather of the car's upholstery, too distraught even to speak. What a fool she'd been, she realised bitterly—she'd truly believed he'd felt the same passion that had coursed through her veins like a flash flood. But all the time he'd been coolly calculating what was most likely to get back to Ralph. His cruelty was beyond belief.

In a different mood she'd have found St Helier fascinating, she thought dully as she walked at Marc's side through the capital's busy and colourful pedestrian precinct with its charming array of flowers and shrubs, liberally dotted about the place in pots and containers. Its atmosphere was definitely European, she decided, spotting several bistro-style cafés with outside dining areas. If she'd been with Ralph right now she'd probably have suggested stopping at one to sip coffee and lazily watch the world go by. Somehow she didn't think Marc would appreciate the idea, she decided ruefully.

'Is it very old?' Tired of the silence becoming ever more weighty and oppressive between them, she turned to Marc curiously. 'St Helier, I mean.'

'Parts of it are. It originally grew up around a parish church, and that's supposed to date back as far as the tenth century. Most of the island's important buildings are here,' he went on, 'and of course Jersey's international banking and finance industry is centred in St Helier.'

She nodded. 'Of course. I'd forgotten the island is a tax haven.'

He frowned. 'That's the popular myth. The reality is slightly different. The authorities prefer to call Jersey a low tax area. That makes it beneficial for residents as well as those who choose to use the island for investments.' He shrugged lightly. 'I don't imagine you want a lecture on Jersey's financial structure.'

'On the contrary,' she retorted. 'I'm always keen to learn.'

He gave her a strange look. 'Then I'll buy you a book on it. In the meantime let's get on with finding you a decent pair of shoes.'

Stung by the snub, she'd have happily snapped straight back at him if he hadn't chosen that moment to veer left into a shoe shop. Muttering under her breath, she followed him in, managing only with a very real effort to summon up a smile for the assistant who instantly stepped forward to attend to them. Less than ten minutes later they left the shop again, Tessa carrying a carefully wrapped box beneath one arm. As they walked back along the precinct towards the car park, Marc glanced down at her, his expression a mixture of amusement and surprise.

'Do you always make up your mind so quickly?' he asked quizzically.

She looked back at him through suspiciously narrowed eyes, wondering what was coming next. 'Why?'

'No reason. I've simply never seen a woman select something so fast.' His smile held just a tinge of self-mockery. 'I was bracing myself for a long and laborious trawl through the shoe shops of St Helier.'

Tessa shook her head, unable to suppress a fleeting sensation of triumph. At least she could surprise him in something. 'I don't see any point in dragging things out just for the sake of it,' she said crisply. 'When I see something I want, I go for it. Why hunt around for alternatives if you're sure you like something straight away.'

He seemed to ponder that one for a moment. 'Does that also apply to men?'

She was surprised by the apparent *non sequitur*. 'I thought we were talking about shoes.'

'We were. But it seems to me you could adopt the same principles.'

'I suppose you could,' she conceded.

'Then why didn't you? With Ralph?'

She whirled round on him then, her blue eyes blazing. 'I knew you were trying to set a trap for me! For heaven's sake, will you never believe me? Ralph and I didn't see each other in that way. We were never lovers because I don't think the idea ever even occurred to either of us.'

'Then why did he give you the bracelet?'

Tessa gave a heavy sigh. 'So we're back to that

again? I don't know why he gave me the bracelet — and I'd never have accepted it if I'd known its true worth. He knew that too. But he'll have to tell you so himself, because it's clear you'll never accept a word I say. Now. . .' she planted both hands on her hips, glaring into his amber eyes, 'can we go back to your house please? I'm tired.'

'You do look rather pale. Must have been your midnight mountaineering.'

She began to give him a blistering retort then changed her mind. There was really no point, she thought wearily. She was too tried to argue any more, too tired and too dispirited, longing to simply lay her exhausted body down on a soft bed for a little while. However, it seemed Marc had other ideas.

'Since we're here, you might as well see a bit more of the place,' he said.

'You mean you might as well drag me round the town some more in the hope that Ralph will get to hear about it,' she retorted cuttingly.

He shrugged. 'Whatever.'

'Very well.' Right at this moment she wasn't in the mood to be a tourist, but maybe it wasn't such a bad idea after all. The sooner Ralph got to hear that she was on the island, the sooner he must surely turn up and then she'd be able to get herself out of the tangled mess she'd inadvertently landed in.

As it turned out, she quite enjoyed the tour of St Helier, Marc proving to be an interesting and informative guide.

'This was the town's market place for centuries,' he told her as they entered the Royal Square. 'All the country folk brought their produce here to sell. However. . .' His expression became faintly grim. 'It wasn't always so peaceful. Two women were executed as witches here, and others were subjected to public punishment.'

Tessa gazed about her, fascinated by the glimpse into the square's history. Then a statue of a Roman emperor, its head wreathed in laurel, caught her eye. 'Who's that?' she asked quizzically. 'Julius Caesar?'

'Not quite.' Amusement tugged at the corners of his mouth. 'It's George the Second. He gave Jersey two hundred pounds to help with the building of an important harbour, and the statue was erected in commemoration. All the distances in the island are measured from the statue, so it's really quite an important monument, which would no doubt please the old king if he knew about it.'

If she'd been tired before, she was absolutely exhausted now, she reflected as they finally returned to the house some time later. The tour of St Helier had been enjoyable, she couldn't deny it, but it had sapped her of what little energy she had left, making her feel completely deflated, like a balloon suddenly emptied of air.

'So help me, Ralph,' she muttered as she reached the sanctuary of her bedroom and collapsed with a groan of relief on to the bed, 'when you finally turn up, I'm going to. . .' Her voice faded away as she plummeted unresisting into the comforting depths of sleep. Some hours later she came to, her eyes opening then creasing confusedly with the notion that something wasn't quite right. Glancing downward, she frowned, realising she was now lying beneath the bedclothes. She could have sworn she'd been lying on top of the bed earlier. Had she crawled beneath the covers in her sleep? She wriggled slowly to a sitting position and her blood ran cold. She'd definitely been wearing a shirt and a pair of shorts when she'd closed her eyes—now she was clad in a lacy white nightdress. What there was of it, she thought disparagingly, lifting the quilt and discovering it barely skimmed the tops of her thighs. Another little something from the wardrobe of the unknown guest, no doubt—in this case, a very little something, she reflected sourly, wondering if Marc had seen the woman parading in it. Come to that—had he seen Tessa? She blanched at the very idea, then shook her head abruptly. It must have been Jeanne the housekeeper who'd undressed her, she decided resolutely. Even Marc couldn't presume so far while she was unconscious. Could he? Then she gave a hollow groan—he was capable of just about anything, and she knew it.

The sound of tapping on the door sent her scurrying for cover beneath the quilt before calling out, 'Come in.'

'So you're awake at last.' Marc walked into the room, bearing a tray. 'I was seriously beginning to wonder if you'd lapsed into a coma. Do you always sleep so deeply?'

'Did you undress me?' The very question brought a warm flush to her cheeks and she glowered at him resentfully.

'I've brought you coffee. Perhaps that will help bring you round.' He laid the tray on the bedside table. 'It's to be hoped you don't always keel over so thoroughly,' he went on conversationally. 'What would happen if you were on one of your safaris and a wild animal chanced into your campsite? You wouldn't even know it was there till it was too late.'

'Frankly I'd rather take my chances with a wild animal than you,' she shot back furiously.

'Why?' He glanced down at her, his expression unimpressed. 'What's wrong, sweet Tessa—are you afraid I allowed my animal lusts to overcome me while you slept so peacefully?' He sat down on the bed and planted one hand on the far side of her, his eyes challenging.

'Don't be. . .' She stopped dead in mid-protest, her eyes widening incredulously. 'You didn't. You couldn't have!'

'Couldn't I?' His carved mouth quirked into a grin. 'Why not?'

'Because even you couldn't stoop so low,' she sputtered.

He gave an indifferent shrug. 'Perhaps. Perhaps not. But if I didn't take advantage of the situation, it was for one reason and one reason only.'

'Which is?' As he leaned over her, the breath caught in her throat. It could only be because she'd just woken up, but she was heady with his nearness, the clean male scent of him filling her senses.

'Which is—that when I make love to you, my pretty Tessa, I want you to be fully awake and participating.'

She drew her breath in sharply, her features contorting with rage. 'That will never happen,' she swore, refusing to let herself remember how much she'd wanted to make love with him just a few short hours ago. 'You'd have to take me by force.'

'You really think so?' Unperturbed, he leaned closer still till his mouth was mere inches from her own. 'So if

I were to touch you now, kiss you now as I did at the zoo, you would be entirely unaffected?'

'Entirely.' But the single word ended in a groan that was part despairing, part longing as he closed the tiny gap between them and pressed his lips to her throat. Helplessly her head arched back and her hands slid up to bury themselves in his dark hair even as she silently commanded them to be still. For long seconds she fought herself, willing her fingers to pull his head away, but as his mouth moved lower on to her shoulder and he pushed the ribbon strap of the nightdress away she knew she was lost. Lost to a raging storm in her blood, lost to pure sensation as his hand found her naked breast and cupped its fullness, his thumb grazing delicately over her nipple.

Nothing mattered any more, not the need to find Ralph, not the fact that she was here against her will, not the shaming fear that he'd undressed her as she lay oblivious. All external reality silently took wing and flew, leaving only the need building up within her, hot and fierce like the lava in a bubbling volcano.

She felt his breath on her breast and her fingers twisted in his hair, pulling him closer. He moved fractionally and she moaned a protest against his leaving, but he simply threw back the quilt with one careless hand and lay along her, his weight pressing her into the mattress. Now she could feel him, hard and exciting, and she exulted in knowing he was affected too by the heat generating into an inferno between them.

His hand moved to her knee and slid along the satin skin of her thigh, and it was with a distant sensation of amazement that she realised the soft sounds of whimpering were coming from her own throat. He lifted her in his arms and pulled the nightdress over her head, and she revelled in her own nakedness. Beyond sense now, beyond anything but the longing to be closer still to him, she slipped her hands beneath his sweatshirt, her fingers cleaving to the taut muscles rippling beneath his skin.

'Tell me what you want, Tessa.' His voice, low and husky, whispered over her skin and her eyes were clouded as she gazed back at him. But even with need growing to fever pitch, the words stuck in her throat, blocked by some lingering shyness. She shook her head, her eyes begging him to understand.

'I can't.'

'You must. Tell me what you want me to do.'

She swallowed hard, one part of her hating him for pushing her to surrender still more than she had already, but another part recognising the liberation such surrender would achieve—a freedom from the paralysing force of her own inhibitions. It took everything she had, but she forced herself to look into his lion eyes, even as the colour drained from her face.

'I want you,' she whispered. 'I want you to make love to me.'

Triumph glittered briefly in his eyes. 'So I won't have to force you?' he said softly. 'You're asking me to make love to you of your own free will?'

Her heart seemed to stop beating as realisation sliced into her like a poison-tipped arrow.

'My God,' she breathed. 'You callous, unfeeling bastard! Are you doing this to prove a point?'

He shrugged. 'If I am, it appears I've been successful.'

In one swift movement, fuelled by the blinding pain of betrayal, she pushed him away and slid from the bed, uncaring that she was naked. After all he'd put her through it hardly seemed to matter any more.

'Please leave,' she said tightly. 'I can't take any more.'

'Oh, I think you can,' he returned evenly as he slowly got to his feet. 'I think you can take a great deal more—and give it too. And you will—when we make love properly. Which we will, sweet Tessa,' he cut into her angry exclamation. 'When the time is right, we will. Now——' he glanced at his watch '—I suggest you have a shower and rifle through that wardrobe again. We're dining out tonight and the *maître d'* doesn't appreciate tardy diners.'

As he reached the door a new thought apparently struck him and he turned back. 'By the way,' he said blandly, 'it was Jeanne who undressed you. But thank you for letting me see what I missed by not doing it myself.'

Driven to madness by his cool words, she reached out blindly, seeking something, anything to hurl after him. Her hand found the filmy material of the nightgown—but even as she threw it, he closed the door behind him and it fluttered harmlessly to the floor.

# CHAPTER SIX

THE restaurant was small, and had a warm, friendly atmosphere, but it was far from the expensive, exclusive venue she'd anticipated. So he'd managed to surprise her all over again, Tessa thought resignedly. Well, that was becoming par for the course. The day she managed to predict Marc's actions with any degree of accuracy, the moon would probably fall from the sky to land in her lap.

'Is anything wrong?' he asked mildly, seeing her frown faintly as she glanced round the dining-room. 'This place serves excellent French food—but perhaps that isn't to your taste?'

As if you'd care! The words shouted in her mind, but she suppressed them, feeling more than a slight sense of suspicion that he was testing her in some way. Well, that was a game two could play!

'On the contrary,' she returned with a cloyingly sweet smile. 'I think it's quite delightful.' She paused thoughtfully for a long moment as she studied the menu, then raised guileless blue eyes to his. 'I wouldn't have thought this restaurant would be entirely to your tastes, however.'

'Meaning?' It was apparently his turn to be suspicious, judging by the narrowing of his eyes. The sight afforded her a perverse moment of pleasure. It was reassuring to discover she could throw a few surprises in his path too.

She lifted her shoulders off-handedly. 'Meaning nothing really.' She smiled up at the waiter as he poured iced water into two small glasses, then took a sip and daintily pressed a napkin to her lips. He was so aggravatingly certain he had her pegged as a gold-digger, and one with a shrewish nature to boot. It seemed highly unlikely she'd ever manage to convince him he was all wrong, but at least tonight she could show him another side. Even if it required a certain degree of acting. For a moment she considered fluttering her eyelashes, but decided against it. That might be taking things just a shade too far. 'I simply had you marked down as a Beluga caviare and Krug man, that's all.'

'So that's it.' He nodded slowly, his features darkening. 'You think I should have taken you somewhere more expensive.'

'That is what you'd expect from a gold-digger, isn't it?' There was more than a gleam of humour in her eyes. 'But in fact you're quite wrong.' She lifted her hands, ticking the points off on her fingers. 'For one thing I can't stand the taste of caviare—frankly I think it's vastly over-rated stuff. Secondly, champagne gives me a headache, and on the relatively rare occasions I drink at all, I prefer to sip meditatively on a fine old malt whisky. And thirdly——' she paused, relishing the moment '—I'm highly relieved you didn't choose a madly expensive place, since I'll be paying my own way.'

Any other man must surely have leapt in at that point to defend his affronted pride, she thought ruefully, watching his expression closely in hopes of even a flicker of outrage. None came. Instead he smiled faintly.

'I'm sorry,' he said silkily. 'I appear to have lost my place in the script. Is this where I'm supposed to say how refreshing it is to meet a modern and liberated woman, or would you prefer the outraged chauvinist option where I loudly refuse to let you pay as much as a single penny?'

She tried, she really tried to look vexed. But the playful sense of humour which had borne her through so many other difficult situations, insisted on surfacing right at that moment as an irrepressible gurgle of laughter, making her eyes dance with mirth.

'Touché,' she conceded generously. 'I believe that's what they call the biter bit. Nevertheless I meant what I said. I always pay my own way, and I see no reason to stop the practice now.'

'We'll argue about it later,' he returned equably. 'In the meantime, let's order. What would you like?'

She ran her eye over the selection on the menu, impressed by the choice of fish and *fruits de mer*.

'Seafood has always played an important role in the Jersey diet,' Marc commented, apparently reading her mind. 'Which of course is hardly surprising given that our waters are particularly rich in fish.'

'Are any of these dishes traditional island meals?' she queried.

He shook his head with a faint smile. 'Not really. They owe more to the French style of cuisine — though that of course has also influenced us considerably. But perhaps I should ask Jeanne to prepare something truly traditional for you.'

'Such as?'

'Well, although she doesn't practise it very much in these modern times, Jeanne is still an expert in the art of *la vieille cuisine*—old-style cooking. She could serve up a few *boudelots, or fliottes* or even *miquolottes* if you preferred them.'

She wrinkled her nose curiously. 'What on earth are they?'

'You mean you've never heard of them?' The lift of his eyebrow told her he was being playfully facetious, and the shock of glimpsing such an unexpected side to his character did strange things to her insides. He was putting on a show for the benefit of any curious eyes watching them, she told herself forcefully, desperately trying to steel herself against the tendrils of warmth uncurling themselves deep within her.

'No.' She cleared her throat, hearing the huskiness in her voice. 'I'm afraid I haven't. Tell me about them.'

He launched into an explanation of the terms, telling her that *boudelots* were sweet apples covered in dough, placed on cabbage leaves and cooked in the oven, while *fliottes* were made from a special batter dropped in boiling milk and served with grated nutmeg and currants. *Miquolottes*, he concluded were made with left-over dough mixed with buttermilk then fried. If he'd quizzed her on the terms immediately afterwards, she wouldn't have been able to tell him a thing, she realised dazedly, because she'd been too mesmerised by the animation of his features as he spoke, and the way he used his hands to describe the cooking methods. He'd only been talking about traditional Jersey fare, for goodness' sake—yet she knew she was in severe danger of melting away before his very eyes, consumed by sheer longing for him.

With a major effort, she managed to dredge up some suitably light-hearted response when he'd finished talking, and for the duration of the meal they managed to maintain the truce. She was all too aware that beneath the conversation, dark undercurrents continued to flow unabated, the tension she inevitably felt whenever she was in his company lessening not one jot. But at the very least they were managing to behave in a civilised manner, without the usual scathing exchanges she'd come to expect. Anyone glancing over at them, seeing them smiling and laughing and chatting easily together, must surely think they were friends. Maybe even lovers. She was unaware of the wistful look that passed over her features with the thought, but he saw it and his own expression darkened.

'What's wrong, Tessa?' he said abruptly. 'Missing Ralph?'

Since Ralph had been, she realised guiltily, a million miles from her thoughts, she was taken aback. 'What makes you ask that?'

'He is the reason we're here,' he said curtly, and she flinched with the brutal reminder.

'I'm well aware of that,' she returned, hating the faint betraying tremor in her voice. 'I know you'd prefer not to have me anywhere around. However, I feel I should remind you — it's not my fault I'm still here. You're the one who insisted I had to stay. No,' she added bitterly, 'you *ordered* me to stay. I had no choice in the matter.'

'So your much-vaunted friendship with my brother wouldn't have been sufficient in itself to keep you here?'

She glared back at him, uncomfortably aware that

he was running rings around her all over again. How on earth could she tell him she'd been afraid to stay because of the effect *he* had on her? 'Ralph's an adult,' she managed at last. 'I was prepared to accept your assurance that he hadn't been kidnapped, or befallen some other equally awful fate, therefore I can only conclude that whatever he's doing, he's doing it of his own free will.'

Glancing downward she realised she was twisting the linen napkin in her hands and dropped it instantly, knowing his perceptive eyes wouldn't miss such a telling sign of her inner tension. 'Why is it so vital that you find him, anyway?'

'Why?' Marc shot back. 'Would it suit your purposes better to have him stay in hiding?'

'What on earth is that supposed to mean?'

His eyes narrowed dangerously. 'Come, Tessa, you're an intelligent woman — you can work it out for yourself. And I'm sure you have. Janine's a patient soul, but she won't wait forever. Perhaps you're hoping she'll break off the engagement — leaving the field clear for you again.'

Barely able to believe what she was hearing, Tessa closed her eyes briefly. 'I must have done something truly gruesome in my life to deserve this,' she muttered. 'I just wish I could remember what it was.' Opening her eyes she glared directly at Marc. 'If Ralph and I had enjoyed that kind of relationship, we'd have been engaged long ago.'

'Unless of course he never actually asked you to marry him,' Marc pointed out cruelly. 'Perhaps you made the mistake of allowing him to "enjoy" the relationship too fully, without first ensuring a commitment from him.'

'How dare you!' Her eyes darkened with anger as she stared back at him, horrified by the insinuation. Yet even through the pain, one accusing question rose up to mock her — could she really blame him for making such an assumption, given the wanton way she'd behaved in his arms? After knowing him for just a couple of days she'd been prepared — no, she'd been *willing* to make love with him. Little wonder then that he should believe her capable of being free and easy with her sexual favours.

She looked away from his probing eyes, feeling sick to the stomach. The terrible irony was that she could never hope to convince him he was wrong — except by sleeping with him. Then he'd discover her inexperience for himself — but pride alone must surely refuse to let her make love with someone who so clearly despised her. She swallowed hard, fighting back a rising tide of nausea. Pride hadn't helped much so far — how could it, when desire for Marc swamped everything else so readily? The brutal truth was that she was trapped, imprisoned — both by his refusal to let her leave the island, and by his determination to believe the very worst of her.

'I wish Ralph were here right now,' she said through gritted teeth.

'Really?' He seemed bored, indifferent. 'You would find his company preferable to mine?'

There was genuine anguish in her returning look. 'I think I'd find the company of a starving bear preferable to yours,' she hissed back. 'But if Ralph were here at least I'd have the satisfaction of seeing you eat your words. You clearly won't believe a word I say — but you must surely accept Ralph's word.'

'Perhaps.' He eyed her assessingly for a long moment. 'But we won't be able to put that to the test until he turns up. So we'll move on to one of his favourite haunts next.'

'Which is where?' She was too dispirited to argue, even though the only thing she really wanted was to go home and slam the bedroom door behind her. Preferably putting a big sturdy chair behind it for added protection. Though nothing, it seemed, could protect her from the agonising betrayal of her own body. Even now as she looked at him and read only cold antipathy in his amber eyes, tendrils of longing were moving within her.

'He's fond of the nightclubs in St Helier. We'll go there.'

If she'd thought her heart could sink no lower, she'd been wrong. She disliked nightclubs and discos enough at the best of times, finding them too busy, too noisy and usually too hot. And this was hardly the best of times. The prospect of nightclubbing with Marc was enough to make her shudder. The reality proved even worse.

'If Ralph does hear you've been dancing the night away in a disco, he certainly won't leap to the conclusion that I could be your partner,' she informed Marc starchily as they entered one of the clubs.

'Why not?' The lighting had a strange effect on his eyes as he turned to look at her, turning them from amber to molten gold.

'Because he knows how much I hate the places.'

For the most fleeting of seconds she thought she

detected a flicker of doubt in his expression, but it was gone before she could be sure. Probably just a trick of the changing light, she told herself resignedly. Marc Duval was not the type of man to be unduly troubled by something as trifling as uncertainty.

'I'll take that risk,' he said shortly. 'What do you want to drink? A fine old malt, wasn't it?'

She smiled faintly. 'I'm impressed by your memory — however, you may also recall I said I liked to sip one meditatively.' She cast an ironic glance towards the disco floor, already packed with dancers. 'I hardly think I'll manage that here. I'll have a mineral water and lime, please.'

'I'll be back in a moment. Stay here.'

'Aren't you afraid I'll grab the opportunity to disappear?' She couldn't resist the tiny taunt.

'I don't believe even you would be so foolish.' There wasn't the faintest element of threat in his even tones, yet something in his eyes made her shiver. As he walked away towards the bar, she was gripped by sheer undiluted frustration. Would she ever manage to win with him? The prospect grew more unlikely with every passing hour.

'Excuse me?'

Surprised by the voice at her side she turned to look into the eyes of a total stranger. About the same age as herself, he was dressed casually in trousers and an open-neck shirt, his sandy hair and sprinkling of freckles giving him a disarmingly boyish look.

'Wasn't that Marc Duval you came in with just now?'

'It was. Do you know him?'

'Would that I could move in such exalted circles!' He rolled his eyes heavenwards, clearly tickled by the very idea. 'No, I've never met him. But I've heard a lot about him from Ralph.'

'You know Ralph?' In her excitement she clutched at his arm. 'Where is he?'

He was clearly taken aback by the impassioned appeal in her voice, but wary too, his eyes flickering away from her.

'Why do you want to know?' he hedged.

His expression was evasive and she bit her lip, dismayed by her impulsive outburst. If Ralph had sworn friends to secrecy, she might have to tread softly to get information out of him.

'Look,' she said persuasively, 'you don't have to tell me where he is if you don't want to. But please — *please* could you tell him I'm here and I need to see him? Urgently!'

He seemed about to reply, then glanced over Tessa's shoulder and changed his mind. Half turning to see what he was looking at, she understood the reason why. Marc was bearing down on them, his expression thunderous.

'I must go,' he said hurriedly. 'I've got friends waiting for me. It was nice meeting you. If I do see Ralph I'll pass on your message.' And he all but tore his arm from her grasp in his haste to get away before Marc could join them.

'But you don't know. . .' It was too late. He was already swallowed up in the crowd, and she hadn't managed to tell him her name. How could she have been so stupid?'

'Who was that?' Marc demanded peremptorily as he handed her a glass.

'I haven't the faintest idea,' she returned. 'But he knows——'

'Are you normally so familiar with people you've only just met?' His cold, clipped tones emanated disbelief.

'He was just a nice friendly guy, that's all. But he knows——'

'And you felt the need of some nice friendly company, is that it?'

Angered by the insinuation, she glared at him, temporarily forgetting the need to tell him about the message she'd given the stranger.

'It would certainly make a nice change from being with you all the time!'

'What's the matter, sweet Tessa?' he returned mockingly. 'Is the strain proving too much for you?'

'Strain?' She tried to inject her voice with disdain. 'What strain?'

'The strain of being with someone who doesn't simply give in to your every whim. The strain of wanting something you can't have.'

'And just what is that exactly?' She tossed her head back contemptuously. 'Let me tell you something, Mr Marc Duval—you may think you're God's gift to women, and judging by the number of female heads you've turned since we walked in here tonight it seems they're in total agreement with you, the poor misbegotten fools. But I'm not one of their number. And although you're determined to believe money is my prime motivating factor—I can assure you I wouldn't have you if I was paid to.'

'No?' He was toying with her now, she could see it in his eyes, read it in his movements as he took one easy pace towards her and she backed uneasily away, only to come up against a solid immovable pillar. 'Then tell me, why is it that you tremble whenever I come anywhere near you?'

'If I tremble at all, it's out of fear,' she hissed. 'Fear that you're going to touch me.'

He shook his head slowly, his eyes never leaving hers. 'I find it hard to believe that a woman who can roam the world, exploring jungle and wilderness alike in search of wild animals, could possibly be afraid of anything.' An enigmatic smile touched his mouth. 'Particularly men.'

'I'm not afraid of men,' she managed to stammer out, growing ever more hypnotised by the shimmering flecks of copper in his eyes. 'But you're. . .'

'I'm what? Different?' He seemed to consider that. 'Why Tessa? Because I'm the first man you've ever met who hasn't simply bowed down at your golden temple?'

Since she couldn't actually remember meeting a single man who had, and would in any case have run a mile from him, his comment might actually have struck her as funny if it hadn't hurt as much. Why couldn't she just shrug off his words? she wondered distantly, still unable to tear her eyes away from the probing amber depths. Why did his opinion matter so much?

'You seem stuck for an answer,' he cut into the heavy, almost tangible silence. 'Have I hit a raw nerve?'

She managed with an effort to force a hollow laugh. 'Not at all. I was simply astounded that someone of your apparent intelligence could get something so wrong.' She gave a tiny shrug. 'Maybe one day you'll see that for yourself. I almost regret I won't be around to see that epoch-making moment, but something tells me I haven't got enough lifetimes.'

A tiny spark flared in his eyes, but she felt no triumph in the sight. She was tired of fighting, tired of being forced constantly on to the attack, because it was the only means she had of shoring up the pitifully meagre store of defences she had against him.

The truly ironic thing was, that under different circumstances she could have grown to really like him, she realised dully, turning to look through unseeing eyes at the crowded dance floor. When he wasn't engaged in his favourite sport of baiting her, he was terrific company — displaying the sort of dry wit she'd always found irresistible, and challenging her mind constantly with his rapier-like intellect. But if she were to let herself thaw to him, it would render her all the more vulnerable. If that were humanly possible.

'Come on. I want you to meet some people.'

She gazed back at him through strangely lifeless eyes.

'People who might get the message back to Ralph?'

He nodded. 'Of course.'

She trailed in his wake as they made their way round the nightclub, pausing every now and again to speak to people Marc recognised. She did her bit, keeping her head high and a falsely bright smile plastered on her lips. She was well aware of the interested, speculative looks she was receiving, and the blatant envy in the eyes of women as they saw her at Marc's side. Which really was ironic, since he was only using her to draw Ralph home.

'I think we've done our duty now.' As they completed their circuit of the club, Marc glanced down at her. 'Shall we dance?'

She shrugged wearily. 'Why not.'

As caught up as she'd been in her troubled, turbulent thoughts, she'd failed to notice that the incessant beat of the disco had changed to a slower, more mellow sound. Reaching the edge of the dance-floor and seeing couples move smoothly into each other's arms, she turned abruptly, but he blocked her path.

'I've changed my mind! I don't want to dance.'

A wry smile curved his lips. 'I'm sorry, Tessa,' he said, perfectly audibly. 'The music's too loud. I can't hear a word you're saying.'

She deliberately stiffened her spine as he took her in his arms. It was a futile gesture. Within seconds the feel of his hard, powerful body against her own was decimating her resistance all over again, robbing her of even the will to fight. She was tortured by the clamouring demands within her to simply lay her head against his broad shoulder, to feel his heartbeat beneath her cheek, to breathe deeply of his uniquely male smell.

When his hand slid slowly upward from her waist, his fingers trailing over her back to cup her head, she was lost again. Lost in the glory of being in his arms, lost in the joy tinged with agony of knowing this was where she wanted to be, lost in the terrible truth that in Marc's arms she became whole. It wasn't just that her body fitted so well against his, nor that she was able to move with him in perfect, untutored rhythm, nor that everything within her was thrilling to the possessiveness of his touch. She was in the grip of something more primitive—a wild pagan recognition that here was the other half of her own splintered soul.

It was a devastating revelation, one that made a cold hand close over her heart. She was wrong—desperately wrong—she had to be! It could only be that the soft melancholy music, the muted lighting and the embrace of an undeniably gorgeous man were combining to addle her senses. Otherwise how could she hope to go on? In a short space of time, another day or two at most, Ralph must surely reappear. She'd have to go home, and even though it had been all she'd been longing for, suddenly the thought of leaving Jersey tore her in two.

So now she was reduced to lying to herself, she thought savagely. Jersey was a beautiful, hospitable place, but it was the thought of leaving Marc that was so excruciating.

Unthinkingly seeking comfort from the very man who was causing her anguish, Tessa turned her face into the curve of his neck, her lips pressing against a pulse in the smooth brown column. Let him make of that what he liked, she thought despairingly. Then his mouth brushed the top of her hair and she was hard-pressed not to dissolve in his arms. No doubt the absent-minded caress was simply an instinctive reaction to having a woman in his arms, she told herself forcefully, dismayed to find she could be so moved. What had happened to her normally strong, capable personality? He had only to look at her and her powers of resistance lay in tatters at his feet.

She never knew how long they danced, losing track of time as one slow ballad merged seamlessly with the next, her body moving in helpless harmony with his. But at last she grew aware of people beginning to leave the dance-floor, and looked up at him through hazy, unfocused eyes.

'It appears that was the last dance,' he said quietly.

'The last. . .?' She blinked in confusion. 'But we haven't been here very long.'

The faintest suggestion of a smile shadowed his mouth. 'According to my watch we've been here for two hours,' he said. 'Which isn't bad going for someone who professes to hate nightclubs.'

She felt herself colouring. 'The music isn't too bad here,' she got out.

He nodded knowingly. 'I know another club which plays the same sort of music and should still be open. Would you like to——?'

'No!' Startled by the vehemence of her own response, she shook her head. 'I mean, no, thank you. I think I've done enough dancing for one night.' Besides which, if she were to risk staying in his arms a single second longer, wild horses wouldn't be able to drag her away.

He nodded gravely. 'As you wish.'

He seemed strangely distracted as they made their way back to the car, and she wondered at it.

'I could easily have taken a taxi home—I mean, back to your place,' she corrected her slip of the tongue hurriedly. 'Please don't feel you have to stay with me if you'd rather go on somewhere else.'

He gave a harsh laugh. 'Are you in such a hurry to be free of me?'

'No,' she returned simply, wincing inwardly at the irony of his question. 'But you've done your bit for the evening, after all. Ralph must surely get to hear we've been in the nightclub. I thought perhaps you'd like time to yourself. Without me.'

Then she gave a startled little yelp as he stopped dead in his tracks and pulled her firmly towards him. One hand went to the small of her back, the other to her head, and even as her mouth began to form a weak protest, it was claimed by his own. His lips moved against hers, warm and firm, the very unexpectedness of his kiss stealing her will to resist. Feeling the insistent probing of his tongue, she opened her mouth to him, welcoming the invasion as he tasted freely of her sweetness.

When he finally released her she was dazed, breathless, her eyes strangely misty as she looked up at him wonderingly.

'What was that for?'

He smiled. 'That was just to let you know that *I'll* decide when I want time to myself, without you. Strange as it may seem, that time apparently hasn't come yet.'

As much as she despised her own weakness, she couldn't deny the tiny thrill his words gave her, a thrill so intense she was forced to snap back at him, terrified he'd sense the way she was really feeling.

'Heaven help me when that time does come,' she said acidly. 'If the way you've treated me so far means you've actually been enjoying my company, I hate to think what I'm in for when my welcome runs out.'

His lips twisted in annoyance and she was pierced by a shaft of regret, even though she'd deliberately courted his anger. For her own sake she had to maintain the prickly, shrewish attitude he'd come to expect. It was scant enough protection, and next to no good at all when he swept her resistance aside and took her in his arms. But at least it shielded her soft and vulnerable heart. She couldn't afford to let him suspect the true complexity of her feelings — a veritable maze she hadn't even begun to untangle for herself. No, for her own sake she had to maintain hostilities, even though there were times — like now — when she'd happily have let the barriers crash.

Back at the house he turned to her, his expression cold.

'I'm going to have a nightcap. Would you care to join me?'

She shook her head swiftly. 'I'm tired,' she lied. 'I think I'll turn in if you don't mind.'

He shrugged uncaringly. 'Do as you wish.'

Actually she'd have loved a drink, she acknowledged wistfully as she headed for the stairs. A good whisky or a fine old brandy might just have succeeded in reaching the frozen parts of her soul — and might have helped her sleep. As it was, despite everything, she was irritatingly wide awake and seemed destined to stay that way. That was entirely due to Marc. As was every other ache in her pincushion heart.

He was in his office when she wandered down the following morning, gritty-eyed and slightly lightheaded after a night of tossing and turning. Since she could normally have won medals for her cat-like ability to nod off, it had been something of a novelty to find herself staring wide-eyed into the dark night. And not a pleasant one. Reading hadn't helped — for the first time since arriving on the island she'd picked up the novel which had been enthralling her just days before. After she'd read the same paragraph half a dozen times without taking in a single syllable, she'd thrown the book from her in disgust. Finding Marc looking refreshed and rested, his amber eyes clear as they surveyed the outpourings of a computer printer, did nothing to improve her humour.

'Making another million?' she enquired archly. 'Couldn't it wait till after breakfast?'

He sent her a wry look. 'What's the matter, Tessa? You don't seem to be in your normal sunny humour this morning.'

She bit her lip, knowing she'd deserved that. 'You're right,' she admitted candidly. 'That was uncalled for. Forget I said it.'

His look of surprise made her bridle. 'What's wrong?' she said. 'What have I said now?'

He shook his head. 'Nothing. I'm pleasantly surprised to discover you're capable of owning up when you're in the wrong.'

'Well, you're a fine one to talk! I can't recall hearing a single word of apology from you.'

'Because I haven't been wrong so far,' he retorted swiftly.

She shook her head. 'No,' she said, deliberately drawing out the word. 'You haven't *admitted* you've been wrong. There's a difference.'

His grin was unrepentant. 'You'll be the first to know if I ever do.'

'I won't hold my breath.' Glancing towards the printer mumbling quietly to itself in the corner, she asked interestedly, 'Are you working? I don't want to interrupt.'

'No, I'm not. And you aren't.'

'But all this paperwork. . .' She gestured vaguely towards the machine with its neatly stacked pile of pages.

'I'm simply keeping tabs on everything,' he supplied. 'I like to know exactly what's happening even when I don't actually have my hands on the wheel.'

'I bet you do,' she murmured, more to herself than to him. 'So this isn't your main centre of operations, then?'

He shook his head. 'I keep an office in St Helier, though as I told you I'm abroad a lot of the time.' His powerful shoulders lifted fractionally. 'Officially I'm taking a break right now.'

'But it's hard for you to let go of the wheel altogether?'

'Correct.' His expression grew distant. 'I'm hoping Ralph will eventually take some of this on board. Particularly now that he's about to get married. He needs a solid base.'

His words rang bells somewhere in the back of her mind, but she couldn't quite decipher their message. She eyed him thoughtfully.

'Do you really believe he could cope with this type of work?'

He sent her a wry look, hearing the note of incredulity in her voice. 'Don't you?'

'I can't really imagine Ralph in any kind of working environment, to be honest.'

Marc's features darkened perceptibly. 'He'll have to get his hands dirty some time,' he said curtly. 'He can't be a playboy all his life.'

She nodded, unable to disagree. She'd used practically the same words to him often enough. 'It can't be easy for him,' she said musingly. 'Having an older brother like you, not just successful but positively legendary in the business world. Perhaps Ralph's simply afraid he won't be able to match up.'

'Playing the part of the amateur psychologist now, Tessa?'

She stiffened, hearing the taunt in his voice, but

deliberately kept her own tones even. 'No. Simply playing the part of a friend. Ralph has always been in your shadow.'

Marc raked long fingers back through his thick black hair, his features harassed. 'I know that. But I suspect he's actually a great deal more capable than anyone realises—including himself. For some reason he's afraid to put himself to the test, and that's what annoys me more than anything else.'

Tessa sent him a curious glance. 'What is your line of work exactly?'

His eyebrows lifted quizzically. 'Don't you know?'

'Not really. Only what I've heard from other people.'

'Which is what?'

She hesitated, loath to spoil a reasonably amicable atmosphere. Then she gave a philosophical shrug—she wasn't to blame for what others chose to call Marc Duval. 'That you're a pirate,' she said with quiet bravado, echoing the words of Clarke Simpson, the man she'd met on the plane. 'Utterly ruthless and utterly without mercy.'

'And what sort of piratical acts am I alleged to commit?' he asked interestedly. 'According to these "other people", that is.'

Since she'd been anticipating an explosion of wrath or indignation at the very least, his calmness was disconcerting. Little wonder he was such a success in business, she thought absently—his opponents probably never knew exactly what he was thinking or how he'd react.

'Well. . .' Seeing the slight warning glint in his eyes she bit down on her bottom lip, beginning to wish she'd never started this. 'I've heard you swoop on the weak and defenceless,' she said, her words coming all in a rush. 'That you buy up failing businesses to boost your own empire.' She winced, waiting for the tirade that must surely now come. Instead he nodded.

'I suppose that could just about sum up what I do.' His eyes hardened. 'In the opinion of some. So tell me, Tessa—do your informants also tell you what happens to those ailing businesses once they become part of my so-called empire?'

'Well no, I. . .'

'Have you tried to find out?'

She coloured uncomfortably. 'No. I haven't.'

'Presumably because you found the pirate version infinitely more terrible and therefore infinitely more interesting.'

Not liking the way that made her sound, but unable to deny the truth of it, Tessa floundered for an answer. After a long moment Marc shrugged.

'Far be it from me to spoil a good swashbuckling yarn with an injection of hard fact,' he said neutrally. 'I'll leave you with your fantasies.'

'But I'd like to know the hard facts,' she protested.

'Then find them out for yourself,' he shot back harshly. 'For now I have other plans.'

Even though it riled her to be fobbed off so blatantly, she couldn't help but be curious.

'Plans?'

'We're going to spread the net a bit wider. Go farther afield in our campaign to find Ralph.' He favoured her with a faint smile. 'It'll give you a chance to see a bit more of Jersey at the same time. We'll set off after breakfast.'

\* \* \*

Leaning back against a convenient rock and turning her face up to the benign warmth of the sun, Tessa sighed in lazy contentment. It had been, she was forced to concede, the most perfect of mornings. They'd driven for miles, Marc proving surprisingly amenable to stopping whenever she wanted to look at something more closely.

At the chillingly named Devil's Hole, she'd shivered deliciously, fully in sympathy with the terrified souls who'd believed the sounds of the sea crashing through the natural arch in the rock were really Satan calling to his cohorts.

'Jersey has always been fascinated by the supernatural,' Marc told her. 'The island's got a lot more than its fair share of ghosts, not to mention the witches and werewolves. In St Clement there's a huge standing stone—La Rocqueberg—where witches used to cook up the odd love potion for heartsick young wenches, or dish out advice to superstitious farmers.'

Tessa chuckled, even as she felt a tiny tremor ripple through her veins. 'And it seems such a peaceful island,' she said lightly. 'Who'd ever have guessed it could hold such dark and dreadful secrets!'

'Dark and dreadful indeed,' Marc agreed solemnly. 'Don't forget however that the island also had quite a contingent of smugglers. And many of the most gruesome tales of ghosts and witches grew up around their favourite haunts and hiding places.'

'You mean—it was in the smugglers' interests to frighten people into staying away?' Tessa shook her head with a grin. 'I still don't fancy visiting those places after dark!'

Reaching for her camera, she prowled round taking

shot after shot of the Devil's Hole, thoroughly engrossed as she worked.

'Are you intending to put together a book of these photographs?' he asked mildly. 'You've used several films this morning.'

She sent him an apologetic look. 'I'm sorry—are you bored to tears? I tend to get carried away with a camera.'

He shook his head. 'I'm not bored at all. In fact it's fascinating to watch you. You seem very...' he searched for the right word '...professional.'

'And you seem surprised,' she returned drily. 'I would hope I am professional. Photography is my career, after all. In answer to your other question— no, I'm not planning a book. These shots are just for myself.' *And you probably don't even realise that you feature in a good many of them,* she added silently. *But when I leave here, memories will be all I have of you.*

'Why did you choose to specialise in wildlife?' he asked curiously. 'Why not landscapes since you clearly enjoy them. Or fashion?'

She wrinkled her nose. 'I've never been interested in fashion,' she said. 'Which must surely have become apparent to you by now! As far as I'm concerned clothes are just for wearing and for comfort. So I'd find it hard to make any kind of statement with them.' Her eyes grew distant. 'But animals—they're always a challenge. Not just tracking them down in the first place, but capturing the real inner essence of them.' Dropping to the ground at his side, she wrapped her arms round her long legs, hugging them to her chest, and grinned self-consciously. 'Does that sound silly?'

He shook his head. 'No. I've spent a lot of time watching the animals in Jersey Zoo, wondering what they make of it all. Whether they have any idea of what the zoo's trying to do for them. Whether the ones bred in captivity have any idea of where their forefathers came from.' His amber eyes held her, more lionlike than ever. 'You're fortunate to have seen so many in their natural habitat.'

'You could too,' she said impulsively. 'Take a little time away from business—go and see them for yourself.'

'Perhaps. One day.'

Later they drove to the pretty bay of Anne Port, where Marc surprised her by producing a bulging picnic hamper from the boot of the car.

'I asked Jeanne to make this up,' he said as she exclaimed over the hamper's contents. 'I hope you don't mind picnics?'

'Mind?' She turned sparkling eyes to him. 'I love them! My folks were great ones for exploring out-of-the-way places. We used to take off for the day in our camper van, carrying enough food to feed an army.'

'For three people?'

'Three people?' She sent him a puzzled look, then smiled. 'Of course. I'd forgotten you don't really know anything about my tribe. I'm the only girl,' she explained, 'but I've got six brothers.' Her features softened. 'My mother said Ralph made it seven.'

'Ralph?' he returned sharply. 'He's met your family?'

'Met them? He's practically adopted them! He said we were the only real family he had.' She stopped abruptly, the blood draining from her face. 'Oh, Marc, I am sorry. That was incredibly tactless.'

'But truthful.' His expression was unreadable. 'Ralph was brought up by Jeanne for the most part — even before our mother died since she wasn't exactly the maternal type. I didn't realise he felt deprived.'

'I'm sure he didn't! He knows how much you did to give him a secure home life. But he's the gregarious type — he loves crowds and busy places. I think that's why he took to my home so readily.' She smiled affectionately. 'With all the comings and goings there, it's usually like Piccadilly Circus. He thought that was terrific. On top of which, my mum fussed round him like the proverbial mother hen.'

Marc's eyes were strangely bleak. 'Jeanne was never very hot on fussing. She believed young boys should be taught to be independent. And to be gentlemen.'

'So they should,' Tessa agreed readily. 'But they need hugs too. I think that's what Ralph's been starved of.'

'Till he met you.'

She heard the cynical note, but didn't rise to it. 'Till he met my mother really,' she corrected him. 'She's the chief disher-out of hugs in our family.'

He slid her a sideways glance. 'Does your mother look like you by any chance?'

Tessa gave a shout of laughter, rich and merry, unable to conceal her amusement as she saw where that question was heading. 'No, Marc, she doesn't. I take after my father. Mum is short and plump with prematurely grey hair she swears we're responsible for. We've told her to dye it, but she says she doesn't hold with such nonsense.' Mirth danced irrepressibly in her aquamarine eyes. 'So if you're trying to ascertain whether your brother was actually in hot pursuit of a glamorous older woman, I can assure you the answer is definitely no.'

An answering smile tugged at his reluctant mouth as he gave her a considering look. 'It seems strange he's never told me about you — or your family.'

Her radiance dimmed. 'He must have his reasons.'

They sat in silence for a while, enjoying the heat of the sun and the glorious sea views spread out before them.

'What's the big rock over there?' she asked lazily some time later, pointing towards the southern end of the bay. 'Does it have a name?'

'It does. That is the Saut de Geoffroi or Geoffrey's Leap.'

'Sounds romantic.' She narrowed her eyes, bringing the huge projecting rock into better focus. 'Did Geoffrey leap to his death because of unrequited love?'

Marc's answering smile was ironic. 'Not exactly. The truth is somewhat more gory.'

'Go on,' she said intrigued. 'After all the bloodthirsty tales of this morning I'm sure I can cope.'

'Well, in mediaeval times they used to get rid of villains and wrongdoers by simply making them jump from the rock. Of course, they met an unfortunate end, dashed to pieces on the rocks far below.'

Tessa shuddered, finding it hard to equate the tale with the warmth and beauty of the day. 'Is that what happened to Geoffrey?'

'Eventually. But he must have had a benign God watching over him as he took his supposed to be fatal leap, because he survived it. However. . .' he paused for a long moment '. . .instead of thanking his blessings, Geoffrey decided to repeat his miraculous feat.' Marc shook his dark head cynically. 'Needless to say a woman was involved, though history doesn't tell us her identity. But Geoffrey spotted her in the crowd and said he would do the leap "*pour votre beaux yeux*."'

'For your beautiful eyes,' Tessa breathed, her vivid imagination recreating the scene in her mind's eye, conjuring up the rakish, devil-may-care Geoffrey and the shyly blushing lady. 'What happened?'

Marc shrugged. 'The inevitable. Miracles rarely happen and certainly never twice. The poor fool perished as all the others had done before him.'

'Oh.' Tessa felt a wave of sadness for the long-ago Geoffrey. 'And the woman? What did she do?'

He sent her a sardonic look. 'The lady with the beautiful eyes probably dined out on the story for the rest of her life. Who knows—it may even have helped her snare a far more suitable suitor.'

'More probably she died alone and lonely after suffering a lifetime of guilt and regret,' Tessa shot back. 'After all, he died for her.'

Marc was clearly amused by her vehemence. 'I hadn't taken you for a romantic, sweet Tessa,' he drawled.

'What if I am? It's nothing to be ashamed of.'

'Did I say it was?'

'Since you're adamant in your belief that I'm a card-carrying gold-digger, I don't suppose you can even believe me capable of being a romantic,' she said. 'You probably think I'm holding out for the big prize— someone rich and indulgent.'

'And?'

'And. . .' Tessa sighed softly, absent-mindedly running her fingers over the rough surface of the rock she was leaning against. 'I know I haven't a hope of convincing you, but the truth is that if I truly loved someone I'd go in rags for them and live in a cave. Material possessions just wouldn't matter.'

'And I suppose you also believe true love lasts forever?' His voice was almost devoid of expression, yet she could hear the shards of ice running through it.

'Yes, I suppose I do.' Which only went to prove that the youthful infatuation she'd suffered for Dan had been a million miles removed from love, she realised now. She'd truly believed herself heartbroken at the time, but with the objective benefit of hindsight she could look back and see it for what it really had been — no more than the first experimental exploring of a youthful heart.

'Nice try, Tessa.' She glanced up, surprised by the bitterness in his voice. 'And I'm sure a lot of men would be happy to fall hook, line and sinker for such sweet sentiments — particularly accompanied by such a wistful look from such big blue eyes.' He shook his head abruptly. 'But wasted on me. I'm an old hand at seeing through acts. Even good ones. And yours is pretty good.'

She gazed at him for a long frozen moment, too stricken even to lash back. It was her own fault, she told herself despairingly. She'd let herself be carried along by the apparently mellow mood, soothed by the absence of friction between them, lulled into believing they could maybe, just maybe, get along in some kind of harmony. How could she have been such a fool? He'd been setting her up — and now he'd brought her down. Only this time the hurt was all the more savage because she'd been given a glimpse of the way things might have been.

She turned away, tears smarting behind her eyes as she packed the picnic things away in the hamper. And that was infuriating too, since she rarely cried. Indignation was still simmering in her soul as they drove away from the beach in weighty silence, but a few miles further on he surprised her by turning off the road into a stable-yard.

'I hardly think you'll find Ralph here,' she said starchily. 'He doesn't like horses.'

'I'm well aware of that,' Marc returned evenly. 'But I want to have a word with the owner. She's an old friend. Do you want to stay in the car?'

'I'd rather have a look round if that's all right.'

He seemed surprised by the request. 'Do you ride?'

She made a dismissive little gesture. 'Only after a fashion. My folks couldn't afford lessons for me when I was a kid, so I made do with a succession of woolly Shetlands and Highlands on my uncle's farm. But I've always loved horse-riding.'

He nodded thoughfully. 'Go and have a look round, then. I won't be long.'

The owner of the stables turned out to be a stylish but weatherbeaten woman in her late forties—definitely not the owner of the flamboyant gold and black dress in the wardrobe, Tessa thought wryly, mentally kicking herself for even wondering. Why should she care who owned the clothes anyway—it was none of her business, as Marc would doubtless tell her. Leaving the two to talk, she wandered contentedly round the yard, her bad mood evaporating as she stroked velvet noses, and gently tugged on tangled forelocks. The stables held quite a selection of animals, from sturdy natives to a sleek thoroughbred, and she smiled reminiscently, remembering how much she'd longed for a horse of her own as a youngster. It was a dream that had never quite faded away. One day she'd achieve it, she decided—when her wandering days were over.

Some time later Marc appeared at her side. 'Seen enough?' he said.

She sighed, 'Not really.'

'Then perhaps you'd like to go for a ride later.'

She turned surprised eyes to him. 'Could we?'

'Of course. We'll come back in the evening. Riding on the beach isn't allowed until after seven o'clock in any case.'

'But I don't have any riding gear with me.'

'No matter. They can fix you up with something here.'

She smiled, feeling a little tingle of anticipation. 'I'll look forward to it.'

## CHAPTER SEVEN

GIVEN the perilous state of her own emotions, it really hadn't been wise to inflict the sight of Marc on horseback upon herself. He looked superb, clearly a man who'd been born in the saddle, she thought enviously, unable to do anything other than thrill to the sight of his calm and expert handling of the flighty young thoroughbred.

'I hadn't realised you were such an expert,' she said, stroking the neck of her own considerably more placid mount.

'Marc's been riding all his life,' the stable owner answered for him. 'I once thought he'd make it to the top, but that was. . .' she cast Marc a sideways glance '. . .well, that was a long time ago. Before he had to give up competitive riding.'

'What did she mean?' Tessa asked as they clattered out of the yard. 'Why did you have to give up? Did you have an accident?'

His face had an unusually shuttered look. 'It was when my parents died,' he said curtly. 'Running a business doesn't leave much time for other things.'

'Oh.' As the thoroughbred danced away down the lane, Tessa urged her mare into a trot in a vain bid to keep up, her mind buzzing. It had never occurred to her till now that in taking on the responsibility of the business Marc might have had to make sacrifices of his own.

'How on earth did you manage?' she blurted out unthinkingly. 'It must have been an incredible load for a young man to cope with.'

He sent her an ironic look over his shoulder. 'The business wasn't as big then. I've added to it over the years.'

Which was probably a massive understatement, she thought wryly. But then she suspected he'd never go into anything without being prepared to give it one hundred per cent.

'Even so,' she persisted, 'to have to do it all alone.'

'I wasn't alone at first. My father had been in partnership with a friend.' His features grew grim. 'Unfortunately that friendship didn't extend to me. He thought having a green young rookie in tandem with him was the perfect opportunity to feather his own nest.'

The bitterness in his voice made her shudder involuntarily. 'What happened?'

'As soon as I discovered what was happening I kicked him out of the nest.' Automatically checking his mount as it broke into an impatient jog, he frowned darkly. 'He thought he could distract me from what was really happening through the services of his young and very beautiful daughter. He was wrong.' He gave a faint shrug. 'He was just the first in a long line of people to see me as an easy touch because I was young and inexperienced. They were all wrong.' His words were brutally blunt but she instinctively felt the pain running through them, and with that pain came a new understanding. He'd been doubly betrayed—not only by someone he'd thought he could trust, but by a lover too. The understanding brought a new agony of its own—for if his inability to trust had such deep roots, how could she hold any hope that he'd ever change his mind about her?

He'd set his mind against her from the start—because of that blasted bracelet, and because of her unfortunate timing in turning up just after the magazine article reporting Ralph's marriage plans. It was circumstantial evidence that wouldn't hold up in any court, she thought grimly—but, given his cruel early baptism, she couldn't even find it in her heart to blame him for his cynicism.

'That man,' she began tentatively, 'your father's former partner—is he still on the island?'

Marc shook his head. 'His pretty daughter managed to find herself another rich fool on the mainland. Clarke lives there too, no doubt happily leeching off his son-in-law.'

'Clarke?' Her head lifted sharply. 'Clarke Simpson?'

Marc reined in, waiting until she'd drawn alongside. 'You know him?'

'I met him on the plane,' she said grimly. 'I'm afraid he's still a bitter man where you're concerned.'

Marc gave a harsh bark of laughter. 'So he filled your ears with poison about me, did he? I'd have expected nothing else.'

'Doesn't that bother you?' She eyed him wonderingly. 'I mean, he must say the same things to other people.'

He shrugged uncaringly. 'People who matter would make it their business to find out the truth for themselves,' he said. 'I know my reputation, Tessa, but I also know the truth. I have nothing to fear from petty small-minded rodents like Clarke Simpson.'

They rode in silence for a while, Tessa trying to come to terms with all she'd heard. She was confused, mixed up, even a little ashamed. She'd accused him so scathingly of making up his mind about her regardless of the truth—but had she done the same? She'd heard so much about Marc Duval, from Ralph first of all and then from Clarke Simpson and the taxi driver, and they'd all painted a picture of a hard, ruthless man—a pirate, driven only by the need to succeed at whatever cost. She'd always prided herself on her ability to judge character for herself, uninfluenced by the opinions of others. But that ability had been singularly absent in her dealings with Marc. To be fair to herself, that was partly his fault too, she reasoned silently. Since she'd arrived on the island he'd been undeniably arrogant and high-handed, but had she allowed that to blind her to other aspects of his complex character?

She was still brooding when he turned to her a few moments later.

'We take this route down to the beach. It gets a bit steep, but the horses have done it a thousand times. Just lean back a little. You'll be fine.'

Even with that reassurance, Tessa still found her heart in her mouth as they picked their way carefully downwards. Not that she had any real fears on her own score—her mare was quite unbothered by the sheer drop to one side of them—but Marc's animal seemed in permanent danger of dancing clear over the edge. Tessa deliberately kept her fears to herself however, afraid to distract his concentration by talking to him. When they finally made it on to the sand, relief washed over her in waves, making her light-headed.

Seeing her pallor, Marc sent her a sharp glance. 'Are

you all right? There was no need to be afraid—Fleur could do that path blindfolded.' At the sound of her name, the mare's ears twitched and Tessa leaned forward to stroke her solid neck.

'I know,' she said. 'And I wasn't afraid—at least, not for myself. But surely you took a terrible risk riding that hothead down here!'

He grinned uncaringly. 'What's life without risk?'

'That's probably exactly what Geoffrey thought,' she retorted tartly. 'And look where he landed up!'

'And what about you, sweet Tessa? Are you seriously trying to suggest you never take risks? In your career where dealing with wild animals is an everyday thing?'

'There are risks—and risks,' she returned loftily. 'I take all possible safeguards, I promise you. I wouldn't willingly deliver myself up to a passing lion.' Yet if she weren't extremely careful her heart would willingly deliver itself up to him, she thought ruefully, feeling that very same heart twist within her as she watched him gentle the thoroughbred, his hand caressing the animal's glistening neck. What she would give right now to change places with the horse! Feeling her skin grow warm with the force of her own wayward thoughts, she forced herself to smile challengingly. 'Something tells me I might find it difficult to persuade my little carthorse to go very fast, so I don't think I can take you on in a race. But could we go for a gallop along the sands?'

'Certainly.' Amusement touched his eyes. 'But don't dismiss Fleur's capabilities so lightly. She might surprise you.' Then he made a faint clicking noise and was gone, a streak of flame across the golden sands. The vision of man and horse moving with such speed and in such glorious harmony was so intense, so powerful, it stilled the breath in her throat. She could only watch entranced, before realising the matronly Fleur was becoming positively skittish beneath her.

'What's the matter, lass?' Tessa murmured softly. 'Are you missing your mate already? Well, so am I. Let's go after them.' She gave the mare her head and found to her amazement that Marc had been right. Fleur might never match the flashy thoroughbred for speed, but her enormous feet nevertheless managed to eat up the ground as they bowled along. They'd never have held any remote hope of catching Marc, but he obligingly rode in a big sweeping arc to come round beside them.

'OK?'

She nodded with a grin as the horses slowed to a walk. 'Just fine. And you're right—Fleur can motor when she wants to.'

He eyed her consideringly. 'Would you like to take Dante here for a gallop? Feel what it's like to really fly?'

'Dante?' Tessa's eyes widened to their fullest extent. 'I couldn't ride him!'

'Don't underestimate yourself either,' he returned gravely. 'I've been watching you—you're a good rider and you're kind with your hands. Fleur can be a stubborn old devil at times, but you've managed to make her do what you want.'

Would that she could be equally successful with a certain other stubborn devil not a hundred miles away, she thought wryly, aware of a little buzz of excitement as she glanced at Dante, barely breathing hard after his run.

'Wouldn't your friend back at the stables mind?' she said doubtfully. 'I wouldn't want her to be annoyed that I'd been riding one of her best horses without her say-so.'

'Dante isn't one of her best horses,' he returned drily 'He belongs to me. I keep him at the stables to be exercised regularly in my absence. And I wouldn't offer him to you if I didn't think you could cope. Or...' his amber eyes glinted a warning '...if I thought you wouldn't be kind to him.'

'Well, if you're really sure...' a grin of delight broke its way through, making her eyes dance '... I'd love to!'

She slid down from Fleur's broad back, handing the reins to Marc as she automatically bent her knee for him to give her a leg-up. It was something she'd done a thousand times before, but as he placed one hand at her waist to steady her she felt a giddying rush that had nothing to do with Dante. It was ludicrous to be so affected by his touch she told herself sternly as she settled into the saddle, yet her fingers were fumbling as she tried to alter the stirrup lengths.

'Here. Let me do that.' He put one hand on her thigh and it sent a river of flame right through her, even though she knew perfectly well he'd done it only to push her leg out of the way of the stirrup leather.

'I can manage the other one,' she said quickly, glad of the chance to turn her burning face away from him.

'Nervous?'

She nodded. 'A little.'

'That's only natural. But try to relax with him — he'll

respond better that way.' His white teeth flashed in the rare and devastating smile that never failed to dissolve her insides. 'Enjoy! You look as if you're going to the gallows.'

Wanting to get the feel of this very different mount first, Tessa walked and trotted round for a few minutes, then, as her confidence grew, eased him into a gentle canter. The sensation was very different from Fleur's rocking-horse gait, and as she relaxed she found herself revelling in the smooth rolling pace.

'Go on Tessa,' she heard Marc call. 'Give Dante his head. You've got the feel of him.'

Needing no further bidding, she did as she was told, needing no more than a gentle squeeze on Dante's sides to tell him what she wanted. As the speed picked up, a bubble of exhilaration grew within her, sending a sparkle to her eyes and a flush of sheer joy to her cheeks. With a wild whoop, she let the stallion flow, totally at one with him as she flew over the sands into the waves, his hooves splashing through the shallow waters. She felt close to ecstasy, on a natural high, and though Marc wasn't there beside her she felt in a strange way closer to him than she'd ever felt before. Dante was his prized possession, yet he'd allowed her — no, he'd *invited* her to ride the stallion, and that was sweet wine to her heightened senses.

She could have gone on for ever, alone with the horse that seemed so much a part of the man, but at last with a regretful sigh, she eased gently back down into a trot and headed back towards Marc and Fleur.

'That was. . .' Unable to find words big enough, she simply lifted her hands in a gesture more graphic than any verbal description. 'Thank you,' she finished simply.

He nodded. 'You did well. As I knew you would, otherwise I'd never have allowed you to ride him.'

She knew it was juvenile to feel such pleasure just because he'd praised her, but it was there all the same. Her eyes glowed warmly as she gazed down at him. 'Thanks. I'm flattered.' She gave Dante one last grateful pat, then slid down from the saddle, only to give a yelp of surprise as strong arms enfolded her and turned her firmly round. She barely had time to register what was happening before his mouth took possession of hers, his hands sliding down to cup her backside and pull her hard against the unmistakable evidence of his desire.

'Watching you ride like the wind was incredibly exciting.' His voice was husky against the hollow of her throat where a pulse was beating a wild jungle rhythm. 'I wanted to be Dante, feeling your long legs round me, urging me on and on.'

His impassioned words ignited a fever in her blood and she clutched to him, fearful her very bones must surely melt. When he lifted his face from her throat, her lips parted, ravenous for his kiss. There was nothing gentle in their embrace, nothing civilised, and something pagan within her thrilled to the wildness of it all.

If he'd pushed her down on the sand there and then she'd have gone willingly, devoured by a red-hot hunger for his possession, caught up in a storm that devastated every rational cell in her soul. How could she ever have thought herself cold? she thought crazily, but the truth reverberated cruelly back—other men might kiss her and hold her, but none would ever drive her to the very brink of madness as he was doing now.

'I want you, Tessa,' he ground out. 'Damn you for making me feel this way, but it's gone too far. I have to make you mine!'

It was only the sounds of whickering from the impatient Dante that brought her back to her senses, making her lift her head dazedly, shaken to the core by the blistering heat scorching her body where it pressed against his.

'Saved by the horse, I believe.' There was grim humour in his voice and she could only look at him through fogged eyes, incapable of even finding her voice to respond. 'Come on,' he said jaggedly. 'We're going home.'

This time as she rode back along the steep cliffside path she barely noticed its dangers, too caught up in trying to calm the turbulence still raging in her blood to register anything else. At the core of it all was the enduring, unmistakable awareness of her own desperate need for him—a need she could neither deny nor dispel. But she'd been down this road before—he'd brought her to this fever-pitch before, only to leave her alone and bereft. Which could only prove she meant nothing to him—proof she hardly needed, she reminded herself savagely. Oh, he was attracted to her, but she couldn't let herself be fooled. Marc Duval was a stunningly attractive man—he'd probably turned any number of willing women to flame in his arms. She was nothing more in his life than a new conquest.

But even as the thought of those faceless women drove a blade deep into her heart, she knew she was fooling herself. Her need for him transcended the purely physical—when he held her it was as though her very soul was crying out to him. It was crazy, beyond sanity; she'd known him only a matter of days and they'd spent most of that time locked in bitter combat, yet she knew she would leave the island irrevocably changed, simply because she'd known him. She also knew she'd spend the rest of her life regretting it if she didn't savour the glory of making love with him. Just once.

If they talked at all on the way home, she was never able to remember it afterwards, too caught up in her own thoughts to make sense of anything else. She'd made her mind up—or maybe it had been made up for her by some external force, she realised with painful humour. Then unthinkingly she shook her head. This was her decision—she couldn't lay the blame at any door other than her own. She was an adult after all, accustomed to accepting responsibility for her own actions. This was no different.

But when they finally arrived back at the house, it was to see a strange car parked on the gravel drive. Any faint sense of relief she might have felt was swamped by sheer acid disappointment, and it wasn't helped when Marc swore softly under his breath.

'Looks as if we have visitors,' he said drily. 'How inopportune.' He slid her a questioning look. 'Or is it?'

She was left floundering for an answer, suffering agonies under his scrutiny. It was one thing to make a mature and adult decision, but quite another to talk about it in cold blood. After a long moment he nodded, his lips thinning. 'We need to talk, Tessa. Later.' Then he got out of the car and strode towards the house. She leaned back against the leather upholstery, closing her eyes as her heart raced erratically. If she were to be granted a single wish right now, it would be that later might never come.

After a few seconds, feeling marginally more in control, she headed towards the house, hoping against hope that Marc would be ensconced with his guest in one of the reception rooms, giving her a clear run to the stairs. She wasn't at all sure she could face seeing anyone right now, let alone cope with the strain of making polite, empty conversation. Her wish wasn't granted. As she entered the house she saw Marc kissing a ravishingly pretty dark-haired woman, and knew with absolute instinctive certainty that she was the owner of the clothes in the wardrobe.

'Please excuse me,' Tessa said stiffly as she made to walk past. 'I don't wish to interrupt. . .' The words stopped abruptly in her throat as Marc's hand snaked out to catch her by the wrist.

'I'd like you to meet Madeleine Rochel,' he said quietly. 'An old family friend.'

The woman laughed, an attractively husky laugh that grated over Tessa's jangling nerves like nails drawn over a blackboard. 'And soon to be even closer,' she said playfully, smiling coquettishly up at Marc.

'C-closer?' The word stumbled from Tessa's lips before she could prevent it.

Madeleine glanced briefly in her direction. 'Through marriage, she said coolly.

For a moment the hallway seemed to spin about her and it was only Marc's hand holding her wrist that kept her from swaying.

'Are you all right?' he asked sharply. 'You're very pale.'

She shook her head. 'I think I've had too much sun today. I'll go upstairs to lie down.' With a monumental effort she pulled herself together, praying the struggle wasn't visible on her face as she looked straight into Marc's eyes. 'I hadn't realised congratulations were in order,' she said shakily. 'You should have told me.'

He made an abruptly dismissive gesture with one hand. 'Madeleine's talking about the marriage between Ralph and Janine,' he said. 'She and Janine are sisters.'

'Which will make Marc my brother-in-law,' the brunette purred, her full sensuous lips curving into a feline smile. She draped herself languidly against his side, trailing her long, varnished fingernails down his arm. 'Such fun!'

'Fun, perhaps,' he returned drily. 'But only if the errant bridegroom returns.'

'He will,' Madeleine averred. 'Janine may be as yet somewhat untrained in the feminine arts, but she is my sister.' She looked provocativly upwards through long, thick eyelashes. 'He won't leave her alone for long.'

'Look, I hope you won't think me rude, but I really would like to go and rest for a while,' Tessa cut in, unable to stand much more of the woman's posturing. 'It's been nice meeting you, Madeleine.'

Reaching the safety of her room, she would happily have slammed the door behind her, but she was frustrated even in that by the thick pile of the carpet. Instead she flung herself down on the bed, her features taut with a mixture of bitterness and misery. Seconds later she was up and pacing the room like a caged animal, too restless to be still. It was nothing more than pique, she told herself scathingly—she was upset because she'd been thwarted. Deciding she was going to make love with Marc had been a momentous occasion, but Madeleine's untimely arrival had knocked all of that on the head. She should be grateful to the brunette, she told herself resolutely, grateful that she'd been saved from making an absolute fool of herself. So why instead did she feel this sense of agonising loss?

Because she was in love with Marc Duval. With a groan of anguish she sank on to the bed, burying her face in her hands. It was no good—she'd been trying to deny the feelings, dismissing them as pure physical desire, but the veil had been ripped savagely from her eyes with the thought that he was going to marry Madeleine. That had been the single most excruciating moment of her life—far, far worse than finding Dan in another woman's arms.

So what was she supposed to do now? As long as she'd managed to go on fooling herself that what she felt for Marc was nothing more than an overgrown crush, she'd been able to cope. Just. But the prospect of his looking into her all too expressive eyes and reading the truth was unbearable. Well, now that she knew the truth, she'd simply have to call on everything that was left within her to bolster her through what was left of her time on Jersey. And she'd make sure that wasn't long, even though the thought of leaving made her heart ache. Somehow she'd have to convince Marc his plan wasn't working—that Ralph wasn't rising to the bait. Surely even he could ask no more.

She was still lying slumped on the bed some time

later when she heard the sounds of light tapping at her door, and Madeleine appeared.

'Marc asked Jeanne to prepare a light supper for you.' She nodded towards the tray she was carrying. 'I told him you wouldn't want to join us for supper.' She smiled indulgently. 'He's involved in one of his business calls so I thought I'd bring this up for you. Grab the opportunity for a nice little chat.'

I just bet you did, Tessa thought bitterly, but she managed to keep her expression bland as she took the tray. 'That was very kind of you,' she said stiltedly. 'You shouldn't have bothered.'

'No bother.' Madeleine's eyes darted lightly round the room. 'I'm so glad Marc decided to put you in here,' she trilled. 'It's always been one of my favourite rooms.'

'You stay here often?' As soon as she'd asked the question, Tessa mentally kicked herself, her suspicion that she was being led by the nose confirmed by the glint of triumph in the other woman's dark eyes.

'Well, until recently I had my own flat on the island, of course,' Madeleine began. 'But when I sold it I managed to persuade Marc to let me bring a few things here—such as my clothes, for instance.' She gave Tessa an ingenuous look. 'I've been working on the mainland for the past couple of weeks, so of course I haven't had time to start house-hunting. But Marc assures me there's no hurry.' Her eyes hardened momentarily. 'And who knows—perhaps I won't need to move out at all.'

'So the clothes in the wardrobe are yours?' Tessa wanted to sound offhand, barely interested, but the pain in her heart echoed in her voice, making it hollow.

Desperately striving to regain her badly rattled composure, she cleared her aching throat. 'I'm afraid I had to borrow a couple of things. I hope you don't mind.'

The other woman laughed gaily. 'Of course I don't mind! Feel free to borrow anything you like.' She smiled, but there was no mistaking the glint of warning in her eyes. 'Just make sure you return it. Preferably untarnished.'

Tessa lifted her chin. 'I'm not in the habit of tarnishing things,' she said coolly.

Madeleine leaned forward to lay a hand on her shoulder and Tessa was hard-pressed not to shudder as she felt the woman's painted talons curling delicately into her skin. 'I'm quite sure you aren't,' she said in an unpleasantly soft voice. 'But one does grow rather possessive about one's own things, even when they're out of sight.'

Tessa met her gaze steadily. 'Then perhaps "one" shouldn't allow them out of her sight?' she suggested, her cool tones in dramatic contrast to the white heat of anger building within. She wasn't fooled for one minute—she knew perfectly well which 'possession' they were talking about.

'Just because they're out of sight—and indeed, even when they're being used by someone else—doesn't make them any the less mine. And don't be fooled, Tessa dear, you're not the first.' Just for a second her mask slipped to show the true face of the predator, then her perfectly painted lips drew back into a smile. 'But you're a big girl. I'm sure you understand what I mean.'

'Oh, I understand all right.' Completely untutored in the kind of games Madeleine obviously excelled in,

Tessa could no longer batten down on the anger bubbling within. 'But what I don't understand is your need to give me such a warning.' Fiery sparks danced in her aquamarine eyes. 'After all, if you're so confident of ultimate possession, why should you worry about anything I might do?'

Madeleine's nails dug a little deeper and Tessa steeled herself not to flinch away, refusing to give her even that much satisfaction.

'I'm not worried at all,' the brunette hissed back, and Tessa awarded herself a point. If nothing else at least she'd managed to scratch the surface of that perfect veneer. She felt no sense of pride in the achievement — she'd never admired bitchiness and it gave her no pleasure to discover she was capable of holding her own in a cat-fight. However, judging by the speed with which Madeleine was able to recover her falsely sweet smile, she was an old hand at the game.

'I'm so glad we had this little talk,' she said lightly, giving Tessa a little pat on the shoulder. 'But now I must return to Marc. It's more than a week since we last had the chance to be alone together, and I know he does miss me so.'

As she reached the door a new thought apparently struck her and she turned back. 'By the way, Trisha dear, don't worry about my sleeping arrangements for the night. Marc will find a place for me.' The brown eyes gleamed maliciously as she gave a playful little wave of her scarlet-tipped fingers. Then she was gone. As the door closed behind her, Tessa flung herself back on the bed, biting back the pain she wanted to howl like a wounded animal. Madeleine couldn't have made her intentions more clear if she'd spelled them out in lettered building-blocks. She was going to sleep with Marc tonight—she was going to lie in his arms and taste his kisses. While Tessa lay sleepless and aching just a few doors away. The agony of it was overwhelming.

Barely even realising what she was doing, Tessa turned on to her side and hugged her knees to her chest, unconsciously seeking succour. How could he have done it to her—how could he have taken her in his arms and kissed her with such passion when he already had a lover? If indeed Madeleine was the only one, she realised with a stab of anguish. The woman had dropped a very heavy hint that Tessa was simply the latest in a string.

She should be able to take comfort from the fact that she'd discovered Madeleine's existence before making a complete fool of herself, for who knew what confession of love she might have blurted out during lovemaking? No, she told herself brutally, she was wrong to call it lovemaking. To Marc at least it would have been nothing more than sex.

Distraught, she pressed her burning forehead against her knees, feeling the early dull throbbing of a Grade A headache. Right now she would welcome a pain in her head, she thought angrily—at least it might go some way to distract her from the agony in her heart.

# CHAPTER EIGHT

TESSA walked with slow, lethargic steps from her room to the stairs and on towards the library. It had been a long, painful night, but somewhere in the velvet darkness she'd made up her mind. Today she would leave Jersey, no matter what Marc might say. Not that he was likely to say anything — Ralph still hadn't shown up, so Marc's hopes that she would prove an irresistible lure had come to nothing. Madeleine on the other hand *had* shown up — which made Tessa superfluous to requirements on two fronts. So — she would confront him now, announce her decision, then leave while she still had at least a semblance of dignity intact. That her heart lay in tatters he need never know.

She walked into the library intending to use the telephone there to call for a taxi, only to stop in her tracks as she saw Marc. He was standing at the big bay window, half turned away from the room, and she had to swallow hard, inexplicably but unbearably moved by the sight of him there — so still and so alone. Then she steeled herself — there was no sight of Madeleine which doubtless meant she was still in bed, sleeping off a surfeit of passion.

'Good morning.'

She started at the sound of his voice. She hadn't realised he was aware of her presence. Was he also aware she'd been standing there for several minutes, just watching him?

'Good morning.' There was only the faintest of tremors in her voice, to her relief. 'I've come down to tell you I'm leaving. Today.'

She waited for the inevitable acid retort, but none came. After several moments of weighty silence, she tried again.

'Didn't you hear me, Marc? I said. . .'

'I heard you perfectly well.'

'Aren't you going to say something?'

He turned fully to face her, his features devoid of expression. 'What would you have me say?'

She made a helpless little gesture, confused by his reaction—or lack of it. 'I don't know. But I thought. . .'

'You thought I would refuse to let you go?' A mirthless smile played over his lips. 'You thought I would play the part of the chauvinist, thus overcoming your feminine objections and absolving you of any responsibility in the matter? So that you could look back on it all at some point in the future and reassure yourself none of it was of your own making?'

'I thought nothing of the sort,' she spluttered indignantly.

'No?' He crossed the room in a couple of long-legged strides to stand mere inches away. 'Are you really so sure of that, sweet Tess?'

'I'm positive,' she shot back adamantly, desperately trying to ignore the way his nearness was making her heart beat completely out of time.

'So that if I were to lift my hand, like this—and touch your face, like this, you would still stand your ground, refusing to be swayed.'

Since she very nearly was swaying, it was hard to

deny it, but she managed to nod with all the conviction she could muster. 'Of course.'

'And if I were to take you in my arms like this, and press your pliant body to mine—and if I were to kiss you. . .'

Any protest she might have made died away in an agonised groan as his mouth touched hers. This was crazy, she told herself wildly. To allow him to kiss her like this, knowing he'd come straight from Madeleine's arms—had she lost all pride? But even thought was swept away by the flash flood of longing coursing through her and she opened her mouth to him, oblivious to anything but him.

'My God! It really is you!'

The sound of a voice at the door, sharp with disbelief, broke through the haze fogging her brain and she jumped guiltily back from Marc, a rush of scarlet staining her cheeks.

'Ralph!'

He nodded grimly. 'It's me all right. You needn't look as if you'd seen a ghost.' His eyes slid past her to Marc. 'And greetings to you too, brother dear. I'm relieved to see you and Tessa have managed to find comfort together—no doubt bolstering one another through the strain of my disappearance.'

'Where the hell have you been?' Marc's eyes glittered wrathfully. 'People have been worried about you.'

'So I see,' Ralph drawled lazily. 'But not too worried to make new friendships.'

Tessa was struck dumb by his coolness, her vivid blue eyes darkening as she stared hopelessly back at him. She hadn't really known what to expect when he finally turned up, but it hadn't been this—this offhandedness. Unconsciously she lifted a hand towards him. 'Ralph?'

'Quite a few people have told me you were on the island,' he said without emotion. 'But I thought it couldn't possibly be you—not when I heard you'd been seen with Marc in fancy restaurants and nightclubs.' His lips curled coldly. 'Your tastes have obviously changed. Not to mention your hairstyle. It was still long and flowing last time I saw you.'

'As it happens we also went to Jersey Zoo and the Devil's Hole, and goodness knows how many other places,' she shot back heatedly.

Ralph glanced at Marc with a languidly raised eyebrow. 'So you've been playing the tour guide,' he said. 'How very gallant of you. I wonder if you'd have been as keen if Tessa hadn't been quite as generously endowed with good looks.'

'My looks have got nothing to do with this!' Reaching the end of her tether, Tessa took a couple of strides forward and planted her hands firmly on her hips. 'I'm only here in Jersey because of you, you big ungrateful lunk! I came because of your letter—because you said you needed help.'

His expression faltered at that, losing its stoniness, and for the first time since he'd entered the room he looked more like the Ralph she knew so well.

'Look,' he said with a trace of embarrassment, 'I'm sorry about that. But...well I'll explain it all later. This isn't the time. Let's just say I should never have written it—I realised after I'd sent it that I had to sort things out for myself. And I have.' He lifted his chin, gazing with a faint trace of defiance at his older brother.

'I'm sorry if you were worried,' he said. 'I just needed a few days to myself. All that stuff in the magazine and the papers about me marrying Janine knocked me completely off-balance for a while. But it's OK now. And I have asked her to marry me.'

'Ralph! That's terrific!' Tessa's eyes lit up with genuine pleasure, the resentment of a few moments before completely swept away. 'I'm really pleased for you.'

'Thank you.' He took her outstretched hands in his own and squeezed them gently, then turned back to Marc. 'We'd like to make the announcement official with an engagement party.'

Marc inclined his dark head. 'Of course. You can have it here.'

'Janine hoped you would say that.' Ralph smiled a little self-consciously. 'She's waiting out in the hall right now. She said I had to face you by myself first.'

'You mean she wouldn't allow you to hide behind her skirts.' Marc's tautened features showed his exasperation. 'Go and get her, for goodness' sake.'

Janine was small and slender with the delicate prettiness of a Dresden china doll—but Tessa wasn't fooled by her fragile looks, sensing the young woman's inner strength. And that was just as well, she acknowledged silently. Ralph needed someone strong as well as beautiful. That Janine adored him was obvious from the way her eyes returned to him time after time, but she knew him well too, that was equally clear from the faintly wry way she smiled at things he said. It would be a good match, Tessa decided, pleased for her old friend.

'Thank you for allowing us to have the party here,'

Janine smiled at Marc, then stretched up on tiptoe to plant a kiss on his cheek. Tessa watched, rigidly steeling her features to remain impassive even as a tiny dart pierced her heart. She wasn't jealous of the girl, just wistfully envious that she should be so easily and unthinkingly affectionate with Marc. If Tessa lived to be a thousand it was doubtful she'd ever be able to touch him so lightly without falling apart inside.

But she'd never touch him again in any way, she remembered now with a sinking heart. The prodigal son had returned, and whatever problems he'd needed help with had apparently disappeared. There was no need for her to stay on the island a second longer. And even though she'd come downstairs that morning fully prepared to tell Marc she was leaving, the prospect dulled everything within her, robbing her of her very enthusiasm for living.

Indeed, a part of her life had come to an end, she realised dispiritedly a short while later as she reluctantly stood at Marc's side at the front door to see the engaged couple away. It wasn't simply that Ralph now had Janine, she thought, forcing a smile to her lips as she waved—she couldn't be happier that he'd found love with such a sweet girl—but their own friendship must inevitably change now, and she couldn't help but feel a faint sadness for that.

'Well.' Taking a deep breath she turned to Marc as the car disappeared down the drive. 'That's that. And all's well that ends well, as they say.'

'And what exactly has ended?' he regarded her gravely.

'My stay on the island, of course,' she said swiftly,

afraid those perceptive, probing eyes would see too much. She managed to shrug dismissively. 'There's clearly no need for me to be here any longer.'

'So Ralph's the only reason you've stayed.'

She shot him an astonished look. 'Ralph—plus the fact that you refused to let me go.'

He smiled faintly. 'Do you have an assignment waiting for you?'

Unthinkingly she shook her head. 'Not straight away, but. . .'

'Then you must stay for the engagement party.'

'No!' The word shot from her lips, the prospect of watching Marc and Madeleine together at the party too much to cope with. 'I mean—thank you for the kind invitation. I really must decline.'

'You've just admitted there's no pressing need for you to get back.'

She took a deep breath. 'Perhaps not, but I feel I've outstayed my welcome here.'

'I thought Ralph was supposed to be your best friend.'

She shot him a suspicious look. 'And I thought you were afraid I'd try to come between them.'

His expression didn't alter. 'I think you know me well enough by now not to chance it,' he said. 'So stay—celebrate Ralph's happy occasion.'

It was no good. Every grain of sense she still possessed was telling her to get out now while the going was still good—but sense had played a lamentably small part in her dealings with Marc thus far, and it seemed it wasn't about to bail her out now. As she looked into his lion eyes, she knew she couldn't leave. Not when he was asking her to stay.

'Very well,' she said heavily, feeling as though she'd just watched the ink dry on her own death warrant. 'I'll stay for the party. But no longer.'

Over the next few days she stayed out of Marc's way as much as was humanly possible, rising early and slipping out of the house before he was even awake, walking for miles along beaches and cliff paths, avoiding the busy tourist haunts in her need for solitude. She was like a wounded animal, needing space and time alone to heal, she thought dismally as she gazed out over the beautiful vista of Petit Port, one of the island's less frequented bays. Knowing she'd never visit the island again, she deliberately went to places she hadn't already seen with Marc, in the vain hope of having at least a few memories untouched by him. Finally, on the day of the party itself, she went on a reluctant shopping trip to St Helier. It must be years since she'd bought a party dress, she reflected, running her eye over a row of glittery numbers in one of the town's many excellent clothes shops. She'd fully intended to buy something quiet and subdued, something that would allow her to merge into the background at the party. But she'd reckoned without a merry-eyed shop assistant who pounced on her as she held up a dark blue cowl-necked dress, mentally assessing its cover-all possibilities.

'No, no, no! This is not the right one for you at all!'

'You think not?' Charmed despite herself by the tiny woman's fluttering hands and strongly accented voice, Tessa couldn't help but smile.

'Certainly not! For one so tall and graceful, we must have something stylish, something to knock the eyes out, yes?' She prowled round Tessa, blatantly assessing her figure. 'What sort of occasion are you dressing for?'

'For an old friend's engagement party,' she supplied. 'But frankly I'd rather have something that didn't even dent the eyes, never mind knock them out!'

The assistant frowned reprovingly, then gave an undestanding nod. 'It is the engagement party of a former lover?' she hazarded. 'This is why you want not to be noticed—so you can cry all alone in a corner?'

'No,' Tessa returned decisively. 'I won't be crying in any corner. But you're right about my not wishing to be noticed.' Then somehow, drawn out by the other woman's interest, she found herself telling the whole sorry tale, albeit leaving the identities blank. The assistant pursed her lips sympathetically as Tessa reached the end of the story.

'Men! Sometimes they can be such fools! Yet where would we be without them?' She gave a very Gallic shrug, then eyed Tessa determinedly. 'So—you must not go to this party intending to be a—how do you say it—a shrunken violet? I personally will not allow it. You will be tall and proud and this man for whom you secretly yearn will look at you and see no one else in the room. No. . .' She held up an imperious hand as Tessa tried to laughingly protest. 'Not another word, I beg of you. Now. I shall take you to a dressing-room and bring garments I have personally selected.'

If she were always guaranteed such expert supervision, she might just begin to enjoy shopping, Tessa decided dazedly as she left the shop two hours later. The assisant—Anne—had been scolding, supportive, downright bossy, and altogether thoroughly enjoyable company. She was also one heck of a saleswoman, as evidenced by the collection of bags Tessa was now carrying away, having bought not only a dress, shoes and underwear for the party, but also several other outfits. Well, despite the chunk it had taken out of her savings, it had been worth it, as a therapeutic experience apart from anything else. She'd entered the shop feeling downcast and downhearted—now a spring was back in her step. Almost.

That evening though, a she prepared for the party, Tessa suffered a severe confidence setback. It was one thing for the redoubtable Anne to tell her she should be tall and proud and eye-catching, but quite another for Tessa to carry it off. As she stepped into a slinkily sensuous teddy and smoothed stockings over her long legs, she was regaled by a fresh wave of doubts. Anyone would think she was dressing for her own engagement party in this get-up. Or at least preparing for an evening with a lover.

Was it too late to back out? Couldn't she simply plead a sick headache and spare herself the inevitable trauma? After all, why should she subject herself to what could only be an evening of torture? She'd almost convinced herself it was the only sensible thing to do when she heard a light tapping on the door and looked around wildly for something to cover herself with. The last thing she needed was for Marc to catch her looking like this.

'Don't panic, it's only me!' Madeleine popped her head round the door without waiting to be invited to enter, her eyes widening as they lit on Tessa. 'My, my! Marc's obviously told you he's invited one or two of his business associates along tonight. Alone.' Her tone was light but there was no mistaking the snide insinuation in her words, nor the glint of hostility in her dark eyes.

'Did you want something?' Tessa asked bluntly.

Madeleine wagged a finger chidingly. 'Now, now, no need to be so tetchy. Although I can understand your feelings in the circumstances. This is after all, very much a *family* affair,' she said, laying heavy emphasis on the word. 'I imagine you must be feeling rather *de trop*. I know I would be, but then. . .' she laughed girlishly '. . .I would never be foolish enough to get into a situation where I patently wasn't wanted. However, since you are here — I thought I'd just pop up and see what you've decided to wear tonight.' She paused delicately. 'Knowing your rather idiosyncratic taste in clothes, I thought I might be able to offer something more suitable from my own wardrobe.'

Tessa gritted her teeth. The woman really was a cat. But she wasn't about to let herself stoop to the same low levels.

'That was very kind of you,' she said briskly. 'But as you can see there was no need. I went into town today especially to buy a dress for tonight.' She waved one hand towards the bed where the dress was laid out in readiness. Madeleine swooped forward, her eyes narrowing in scrutiny.

'So you're going to be the lady in red tonight,' she said at last with a forced smile. 'The scarlet woman — how singularly appropriate. And how very daring of you to wear something so lacking in subtlety.' As she turned back to face Tessa there was open malice in her eyes. 'But don't countenance any foolish hopes that Marc will be won over by this,' she hissed. 'If things go according to plan, I intend tonight's celebrations to be not just for one engagement between the Duvals and the Rochels—but two!' Then she swept out of the room, leaving behind only the scent of her heavy, rather cloying perfume.

Tessa sank down on the bed, her knees suddenly buckling beneath her. If Madeleine was telling the truth, the evening was going to be an even greater ordeal than she'd feared. And why shouldn't she be telling the truth? Tessa realised with anguish. She might be a bitch, but she was a supremely attractive one, not to mention sophisticated and elegant. And maybe that was what Marc really needed in a wife, she thought desolately. Having a woman like Madeleine on his arm could only be an asset in his high-flown business circles—whereas a wildlife photographer with a natty line in safari shorts would be nothing but a liability.

She glanced at her watch and groaned heavily. Time was marching on relentlessly—if she didn't get a move on she'd be forced to walk into the party late, and despite Anne's advice, the last thing she wanted was to draw attention to herself by making an entrance. But she had to go—she owed it to Ralph and all they'd been to one another.

A short while later she faced herself in the bedroom's full-length mirror, unable to resist an ironic little smile as she surveyed her own reflection. Tonight she was beautiful. The vivid scarlet dress moulded her willowy figure to perfection, giving sweet emphasis to her gentle curves, and lending a much-needed glow to her uncharacteristically pale features. Despite the fact that she'd applied the make-up Anne had bullied her into buying with a shaky hand, she'd done it well, making her eyes larger and more lustrous than ever, her generous mouth lusciously inviting.

Anyone looking deeper must surely see the shadows haunting those aquamarine depths, and the wistfulness lingering in the curve of her lips. But she wouldn't give anyone the opportunity to look deeper, she decided resolutely—particularly Marc. Tonight she would be a veritable butterfly, never settling anywhere for long.

And she did her best. From the moment of joining the family party for a pre-party cocktail as she'd been bid earlier, she put on an act worthy of any Oscar. The sight of Marc, heart-twistingly gorgeous in jet-black evening suit and white shirt, nearly brought her to her knees before the evening had even begun, but ironically enough it was the threatening look Madeleine sent in her direction that gave Tessa the strength to go on. She smiled, she laughed, she listened interestedly and conversed animatedly, and only her unnaturally bright eyes betrayed the fact that she was being torn apart inside.

Since the house, large as it was, didn't possess a ballroom as such, the party proper managed to ramble through several different rooms and that suited her well, since it meant she could flit from place to place, a vivid, restless flame.

'Come and dance with me.'

'Why, certainly, I. . .' The words died on her lips as she turned with a polite smile, to find Marc at her side. She'd been so caught up in swiftly checking out the room to ensure he wasn't in it, she'd forgotten to watch the door. He must have come in just after her, she thought wildly, the mask of her composure in severe danger of cracking.

'You've been avoiding me all evening,' he said in a low voice as he took her elbow and propelled her towards the dining-room which had been cleared for dancing.

'Don't be silly!' She tried for an airy little laugh, praying its faint tremor was audible only to her own ears. 'Why should I do that?'

'You tell me,' he returned grimly. Reaching the dining-room, he pulled her rigid form into his arms and she steeled herself, willing her treacherous body not to melt as it usually did as soon as it came into contact with his. It was a lost cause. 'Come on, Tessa. What sort of game are you playing? I've barely seen you for the past few days.'

She tried to shrug dismissively, but the action only served to push her already sensitised breasts against his hard chest. 'You clearly had your hands full with family matters,' she said breathlessly. 'I didn't want to intrude where I wasn't wanted.'

'Not wanted?' he echoed. 'My God, Tessa. . .' Words seemed to fail him and he slid his hands down her back, pulling her more firmly against him. The evidence of his need burned against her, lighting an answering fire somewhere deep in the pit of her stomach, and she closed her eyes helplessly. 'Can't you feel what you're doing to me? Feel the hunger in me, Tessa—then tell me you're not wanted.'

'You may want my body,' she whispered brokenly, 'But I can't. . .'

'Can't what?' he shot back jaggedly. 'Can't bear to make love with me? Why not—is the idea really so repugnant to you?'

He was so far off the mark, a wave of hysteria swept

over her. She was walking a knife-edge, perilously close to cracking, staring into an empty abyss as the ill-fated Geoffrey had done so long ago. But at least Geoffrey tried, a tiny voice murmured provocatively in her mind. His wild impulsive gesture cost him his life — but at least he had courage enough to dare. All she had done was back away, unable to admit how much she wanted Marc, absolving herself of all responsibility when she melted in his embrace. If she had made love with him, she'd have been able to look back and say, 'He swept me off my feet. I wasn't strong enough to resist him.' But that wasn't good enough. Not now. Now she owed it to herself — and maybe even to the memory of the long-ago Geoffrey, to make that leap of faith into the dark unknown. Whatever the cost.

Lifting her head, she looked deep into his penetrating eyes.

'No, Marc,' she said softly. 'The idea of making love with you isn't repugnant to me. In fact I. . .'

'Are you two going to stand there swaying together all night?' A loud jovial voice shattered the moment and Marc's dark brows drew thunderously together. The newcomer, a middle-aged man with a paunch threatening to spill over the straining waistband of his trousers, slapped him on the back. 'Sorry, old man, I can quite understand why you're giving me such a filthy look. I'd be pretty put out if someone interrupted me while I was dancing with such a gorgeous creature.' A smile creased the man's fleshy jowls but failed to touch his pale blue eyes and Tessa felt an instinctive wave of revulsion. 'Anyway, since I'm here,' he went on, turning the full force of his attention on Marc, 'I wanted to ask you how the Brazilian deal was going.'

'Brazilian deal?' Marc's voice was sharp with surprise. 'How do you know about that?'

The man gave him a mockingly reproving look. 'Oh, come, come, Marc—you're not naïve. You know these things can't be kept under wraps, particularly when one has friends in many camps. Which, as you know, I do.' He leaned forward conspiratorially and Tessa caught the whiff of too much rich food on his sour breath. 'Just be careful of the conservation freaks. They may be cranks, but they can do a lot of damage to a deal like this one.'

'I'm well aware of that,' Marc returned with dangerous quiet. 'I can handle them.'

The man guffawed. 'Of course. I'd quite forgotten your interest in wildlife.' He nodded approvingly. 'That was a very astute move, I must say, and now of course I can see the reasoning behnd it.' The pale eyes hardened momentarily to ice. 'You won't forget your friends in this one, will you, Marc? We entrepreneurs must stick together.'

As he walked away, Tessa turned wide shocked eyes to Marc. 'What was that all about?'

'Nothing that need concern you for the moment,' he returned grimly. 'Now—what were you about to say before that ox butted in?'

She was too stunned to respond, her mind whirling. She had to have time to take it all in.

'Will you excuse me, please, Marc?' she said abruptly. 'I'd like to go and sit down for a while.'

'As you wish. I'll come with you.'

'No. I'll be fine. You carry on dancing.'

Wrenching herself from the arms still holding her firm, she turned and almost ran from the room, never stopping till she reached the sanctuary of the library which had been declared out of bounds to the party-goers. There she closed the door firmly behind her and stumbled blindly towards one of the big wing chairs, badly in need of its sturdy support. Sinking into the worn leather she dropped her head into her hands, groaning heavily.

She didn't even know the identity of the man who'd been talking to Marc, yet with a few casually cruel words, he'd shocked her to the core. It wasn't that she'd been harbouring any real fantasies where Marc was concerned—she knew with agonising certainty that his desire for her was a purely physical one—but to discover the true depths of his cynicism was devastating. And this was the man she'd fallen in love with.

Even as they'd argued about everything else, she'd honestly admired and respected his apparent commitment to the ideals of conservation—ideals she shared wholeheartedly. To find out they'd been nothing more than a cover for his true activities was more than she could bear. Yet how else could she interpret what she'd just heard? Marc was involved in some kind of deal involving Brazil which would alienate the conservation lobby. She had no way of knowing what the deal entailed, but Brazil held vitally important though largely decimated rainforests. Conservationists were desperately trying to preserve what little was left of those once great forests, which were ecologically important in their own right, and formed the habitat for many terribly endangered species. But they also held rich exploitation possibilities for the greedy. Could Marc really be involved in anything so reprehensible?

This time she couldn't hold back the flood of bitter

tears, sobs of anguish ripping painfully through her slender frame.

'Tessa! Sweetheart, what's the matter?' There was a soft thump as Ralph fell to his knees before her and she looked up through fogged eyes to see a look of horrified concern on his features.

'Go away,' she groaned. 'Leave me alone.'

'I can't leave you alone. Not when you're like this.' He reached out a hand in a gesture of comfort, but she slapped it away, terrified that the slightest sign of sympathy would trigger a deluge of tears she might never be able to stop.

'Why not?' She deliberately injected venom into her voice. 'It's all your fault I'm here in the first place. And why did you decide to just disappear after sending me that blasted letter? You must surely have realised I'd come to you after receiving such a cry for help!' Under the circumstances the letter was the least of her problems, but she was glad to have it to latch on to. The last thing she needed was for Ralph to discover her heart was breaking because of his brother.

'I'm sorry, Tessa,' he said with real contrition. 'I know I've been a complete idiot. You of all people didn't deserve to be treated that way.' He gave a helpless shrug. 'I was just so confused, so mixed up. I wrote to you in a moment of madness, I suppose — you'd always been there to help me out of every other mess I'd ever gotten into. But when you didn't reply right away, I suppose I thought you'd abandoned me.' He gave a sheepish little smile. 'Stupid, huh? I should have known better.'

'Yes, you should,' she said shortly. 'I didn't reply straight away because I was in Tasmania. Your letter must have been in my house for a couple of weeks before I got it. And I came straight away as soon as I'd read it,' she added accusingly.

He gave a little half-nod. 'I realise that. And if I'd been thinking straight I'd have worked out for myself that you must be away somewhere. But I wasn't thinking straight. So the only thing left to me as far as I could see was to get away and be by myself for a few days.' He smiled faintly. 'Strangely enough, it was the best thing I've ever done. It made me think—really think—for the first time in my life.'

'What did you have to think about?' she asked, more gently now as she recognised the signs of the very real strain he'd been under.

Ralph sat back on his heels, his long fingers splayed out on his knees. 'You know me better than any other living soul,' he said frankly, 'except now perhaps Janine. So you'll understand it when I say I've been a stupid, immature fool who's coasted happily along in life never having to make any real decisions for himself. There's always been someone stronger there in the background to make decisions for me—Marc of course, and then you. In a strange sort of way you've allowed me to go on being a child.'

'Now hang on a minute,' she cut in, 'are you blaming Marc and me for all of this?'

'No, of course not! It's my own fault for not digging my heels in long ago and staking my claim to independence. But I found it easier the other way.'

'So what happened?'

Ralph's eyes softened. 'Janine happened. We've been friends for a long time, Janine and I, so I suppose it was another major shock to my system when I discovered I was in love with her. She made it clear right from the start that she wouldn't be satisfied with a light little no-strings romance. If we were to become involved, she wanted it to be for good, or not at all. And she said that meant trying to make something of myself, because she didn't want a playboy husband.'

'So that's what you meant in the letter about someone wanting you to strive for purer, higher ideals,' Tessa nodded. 'But what about the other part—the bit about selling your soul to the devil?'

He gave a sheepish little grin. 'Perhaps a touch melodramatic,' he admitted, 'but that's the way it felt at the time. I was talking about Marc of course—he wants me to join the family business. Says it's time I learned the harsh realities of life.' He dropped his eyes. 'He's right, of course, but I don't know if I can cope with that sort of environment Tess. Can you see me trying to wheel and deal among the sharks?' He shuddered. 'They'd rip me to pieces.'

'Maybe not,' she said softly. 'But you'll never know till you try. It looks to me as if you've come a long way already Ralph—you've grown up a lot since I last saw you. I believe you can do anything you set your mind to—but if business isn't the right thing for you, then find something else. Only find it for yourself!'

He looked up with a grin, looking more like the Ralph of old, but with a new look of growing confidence she'd never seen in him before. 'That's what I decided on my litle sojourn away,' he said. 'I'm going to give it a year—even Marc can't ask for more than that. And I really will give it my best shot. If it doesn't work out—I'll find something else. But I won't let myself just drift any more.'

'Good for you. Now. . .' she eyed him sternly '. . .at the risk of sounding as though I'm trying to tell you what to do all over again, shouldn't you be with Janine? She'll be wondering where on earth you've got to.'

He shook his head. 'She knows where I am. In fact it was Janine who sent me after you just now — she saw you heading this way and said you looked upset.' His warm brown eyes regarded her perceptively. 'How did Marc upset you, Tessa?'

'He didn't. Don't be silly.' But even as she looked away he leaned forward and took her hands in his own.

'Hey,' he said softly. 'This is Ralph you're talking to, remember? Since when have you been able to lie to me?'

She gave a rueful little laugh but to her horror found it quivering dangerously on the edge of tears. 'It's nothing, Ralph, honestly. Just me being foolish, that's all.'

'Then it is Marc.' He swore softly under his breath. 'I think I always knew this would happen. Knowing the two of you as well as I do, I thought you'd be attracted to one another.' He gave a rueful little smile. 'And the very idea made me jealous as hell.'

'Jealous? But why Ralph? We never had that sort of relationship.'

'I know,' he agreed. 'But for so long I held on to you in my mind as being the one person who was truly mine.' His eyes held hers beseechingly. 'Can you even begin to understand that? It's not that I wanted more of our friendship — I didn't. But you were the only one who seemed to care for me, with no regard to Marc, or the Duval fortune. You were *my* friend, my ally — my sister even.'

'Is that why you never told Marc about me?'

He nodded. 'When I was with you—and your family—I was in a different world. Somehow I just didn't want my two worlds to collide. Besides which...' he gave a little laugh '...I suppose I was afraid if you ever met him you'd like him more than me. Juvenile, huh?'

'Oh, Ralph. You idiot.'

'Was I really so much of an idiot, though?' He eyed her shrewdly. 'When I first turned up, you were in his arms. And here you are now, in tears. I've got a good memory, Tess.' He was frowning as he tipped her chin gently upward to look into her suspiciously bright eyes. 'You didn't look this way over Dan. He hurt you, I know, but he didn't make you look as if your heart was in shreds. You've really got it bad this time, haven't you?'

Unable to stem the sorrow any longer, she dropped her head forward to rest on his shoulder, desperately needing the warmth of his comfort. His arms went round her, his voice murmuring soothingly into her hair. In his embrace she felt as secure as if it had been one of her own brothers holding her close, and just for a moment she allowed herself to lean against him, as she tried to marshal her scattered defences all over again. Then a cold hand clutched at her heart and she pulled frantically back as the door crashed open behind them.

'So I was right all along.' Marc stood in the doorway, his eyes blazing amber fire. 'You just couldn't resist giving it one more try, could you, Tessa?'

'Now wait just a munute, Marc,' Ralph cut in swiftly as he got to his feet. 'You've got this all wrong!'

'Have I?' There was a wealth of scorn in his words as he shook his dark head. 'I don't think so. Now get the hell out of here, Ralph—get back to Janine, though heaven knows, right at this moment you don't deserve her.'

'I'm going nowhere,' Ralph shot back heatedly, but Tessa leaned forward to lay a hand on his arm.

'Please,' she said in a strangely dead little voice. 'Marc's right. You must go back to Janine. This is her night. Don't let anything spoil it for her.'

He looked down at her, clearly torn. 'I don't want to leave you like this.'

Her lips twisted into the parody of a smile. 'It's OK. I'll be fine.'

Ralph's eyes flickered from Tessa to Marc, then back again. 'If he hurts you——' he began.

'What the hell do you take me for?' Marc cut in irately. 'I would never lay hands on a woman in anger—no matter how great the provocation.'

Ralph shook his head. 'That's not the only way to hurt a woman. And believe me, Marc—this one doesn't deserve to be hurt. She's the best friend a person could ever ask for.' His eyes searched Tessa's. 'Are you sure you want me to go?'

She nodded wordlessly.

'Then I will. But I won't be far away, Tessa.' He smiled tenderly. 'I'll never be far away.'

As the door closed softly behind him, Tessa steeled herself for the inevitable onslaught. When none came she lifted her eyes to his and the hairs prickled on the back of her neck as she saw the look of black condemnation there.

'Go on, Tessa,' he said with quiet malevolence. 'Tell

me why you were in Ralph's arms. Make me believe I've been wrong about you all this time, even in the face of such damning evidence. This is your big chance.'

She gazed back at him in mute helplessness. What could she say—that Ralph had been comforting her because he'd discovered she was hopelessly in love with Marc? The very idea was untenable. At last she shook her head despairingly and his lips twisted in disgust.

'You can't do it, can you? Even you can't bring yourself to tell such a bare-faced lie. Though frankly that surprises me. You've certainly been adept enough at lying when you've been in my arms. But perhaps that came easily to you. Perhaps you've had ample experience of doing just the same with other men. Poor suckers!' His eyes grew bleak. 'But then I've been the biggest sucker of all, haven't I, Tessa? I was actually fool enough to find I was starting to believe you— starting to believe all the sweet stories you told me about your friendship with Ralph. I even asked you to stay on for the party, thinking something was beginning to grow between you and me.' He gave a harsh exclamation of self-contempt. 'My God—how blind can one man be?'

Driven to the end of her tether, she leapt to her feet then, her aquamarine eyes wide and blazing. 'That's enough!' she cried. 'You condemn me for being a liar, just because of something you *think* you saw going on between me and Ralph—when all the time you're playing the part of the compassionate and concerned benefactor and plotting to exploit something rare and precious for your own mercenary ends. Clarke Simpson was right about you—you are a pirate. And a hypocrite!'

His lips twisted into a savage smile. 'You haven't the faintest idea what you're talking about,' he said. 'And I'm not going to explain it to you, because frankly you're not worth the effort. I want you out of here—the first thing tomorrow morning. I'll make sure a car's arranged to take you to the airport. And if you have any idea of what's good for you, you'll never set foot on Jersey again. Not while I'm here.'

She was too blinded by tears to see him walk away.

# CHAPTER NINE

TESSA closed the bedroom door wearily behind her and leaned her weight against it, her lashes fluttering down over heavy eyes. Maybe she'd been wrong to come here, she thought dully, but after several weeks of wandering, too restless to stay anywhere for long, the temptation to simply throw herself back into the comforting bosom of her family had proved too strong. But it seemed even here she couldn't find the inner peace she so desperately craved. Every time she saw the anxious look in her mother's eyes, or dredged up a smile in response to her father's kindly questions, she felt guilt that she should be burdening them with her obvious unhappiness.

Today several of her brothers, complete with wives and families, had descended on the place, and if anything they'd made her feel even worse. She was perfectly sure her mother had summoned them home, that much was obvious from the determined way they'd set about trying to cheer her up, and she was touched to the heart by their loving efforts. But the strain of it all had been almost enough to crack her in two.

It was no good, she realised painfully. She'd been trying to run away from the pain of leaving Marc, but there were some things a person simply couldn't run from — because they were lodged inside, locked in the heart. After leaving Jersey, she'd headed for one of her favourite game reserves in Africa, knowing she'd be able to cover the cost of the trip with the photographs she took there. But even though she'd worked diligently, throwing everything she had into it, the resulting shots had been unusable — totally lacking in the subtlety or understanding which had become her hallmark.

Distraught, she'd returned to her own cottage in the Borders, only to discover an envelope bearing a Jersey stamp waiting for her. Sick at heart, she'd been tempted simply to throw it on to the fire without even opening it, but at last ripped it open, to find an invitation to Ralph and Janine's wedding. The sight had brought the sting of tears to her eyes — under different circumstances she'd have dearly loved to see Ralph being married. But how on earth could she go back to the island now?

She still had a painful lump in her throat as she sat down to write a short note to Ralph and Janine, wishing them every happiness together, but saying she simply couldn't be there, and hoped they would understand. Unable to face even the thought of shopping for a wedding present, she enclosed a cheque and asked them to buy something for themselves with her love. Then she sat back with a heavy sigh and closed her eyes wearily. Surely that should be the end of the matter now.

But that evening she answered the telephone to hear Marc's voice, and flung the receiver back into its cradle, stunned to disbelief. Had he discovered that the invitation had been sent, she wondered wildly — had his call been to warn her not to attend the wedding? Well, he had no need to fear. She would be many miles away from Jersey on Ralph's big day. She left the phone off the hook for the rest of the evening.

'Tessa? Can I come in, please?'

She sighed heavily at the sound of her oldest brother's voice. She should have known he wouldn't leave her in peace for long.

'What is it, Tom?' She opened the door to him, her expression one of dull resignation as she steeled herself for the inevitable interrogation.

'Someone's here to see you,' he said. 'Downstairs.'

'Someone to see me?' Her attempt at a smile didn't quite make it. 'I thought the entire clan was already gathered.'

'This person isn't family,' Tom returned grimly, his normally amiable features uncharacteristically taut. 'And if it's who I think it is, I may be in severe danger of knocking his block off.'

She blinked in surprise. 'Why? Who do you think it is?'

'The swine who's made you look like—like. . .' He threw up his hands frustratedly, unable to find a tactful description. 'Like hell!'

'What do you mean?' The breath lodged in her throat, making it difficult to speak. 'Why do you say that?'

'Because he's got the same tormented look in his eyes as you have! Now suit yourself, Tessa—if you want me to throw him out on his ear, I'll be more than delighted to do so.' He cleared his throat gruffly. 'But maybe you'd better come down and see him yourself first.'

'Him?' An erratic little pulse began beating wildly in her throat. 'Did he tell you his name?'

'He hardly needed to. It's Ralph's brother. I'd have known him anywhere.'

Tessa closed her eyes, feeling the room begin to spin around her. Marc was here? He'd pursued her right to the family home? Had the whole world gone completely crazy?

'All right,' she managed to husk out at last. 'I'll come down.'

'Mum's put him in the front room. Said you'd probably want a bit of privacy.' His brows drew together thunderously. 'But I won't be far away. Just you yell if you need me!'

She walked slowly downstairs, feeling as if her feet had lead weights attached to them. Marc was looking out of the window when she walked into the front room, and for a moment she stood in the doorway, barely able to breathe for the suffocating rush of undeniable joy of seeing him. Terrified he'd read the truth of her feelings in her eyes, she deliberately injected hostility into her voice when she spoke.

'If you've come to warn me not to attend Ralph's wedding, there was no need. I won't be there.'

His expression as he turned slowly to face her was beyond interpretation.

'Not even if the invitation comes directly from me?' His amber eyes held hers for a long, mesmerising moment. 'I want you to come to the wedding, Tessa. I want you to come back to Jersey.'

'But you ordered me to leave! Why have you changed your mind?' As he took a step towards her, she backed away, her expression stricken. 'No! Don't come near me! Stay where you are,'

His features tautened. 'My God, Tessa, what have I

done to you?' His voice was so low she could barely hear it. 'Are you afraid of me? Did I really frighten you so much?'

She shook her head, biting her lip painfully. Everything within her wanted to cry out to him, to tell him he hadn't frightened her at all, not in the way he meant it. It was herself she was terrified of — because even as she watched him standing there so tall and strong, she wanted him with every fibre, every cell of her being. Even the knowledge of his treachery in the Brazilian deal meant nothing in comparison to the yearning consuming her.

'Please,' she said hoarsely. 'Say whatever it is you've come to say. But stay where you are.'

'I've come here to apologise,' he said. 'You once said you'd love to be there when I acknowledged I'd been wrong about something — and your wish is granted.' A crooked smile touched his lips. 'I think I've known all the way along that I was wrong about you, but I've fought it with everything I had. When you first appeared at my home, I knew I wanted you. Then I thought you were just another thwarted girlfriend of Ralph's, trying to claw back something of the relationship, and that infuriated me, because I knew how strongly I was attracted to you myself. I deliberately kept that anger boiling and turned it against you, because I couldn't cope with the things you were making me feel.' He shrugged his powerful shoulders. 'It was a form of self-defence, I suppose.'

'Self-defence?' Barely able to believe what she was hearing, she echoed the words incredulously. 'Against me?'

He nodded. 'You made me vulnerable. I can't afford

to be vulnerable, Tessa. I need to be strong. I've always needed to be strong. But. . .' he smiled self-mockingly '. . .as my younger brother has seen fit to remind me, the strongest tree is the one which bends in the wind, not the one which tries to stand up against it. I tried to stand up against all the emotions you stirred up within me, and the effort nearly broke me.' He paused for a long moment, his eyes never leaving hers. 'When I found you in Ralph's arms, I was devastated. But it also forced me to face up to the truth of all you meant to me. I drove you from the island because I was afraid if you stayed I'd never be able to let you go. And I had no idea of how to cope with that sort of needing.

'When you wrote back to Ralph, refusing the wedding invitation, he was concerned about you — oh, he didn't tell me so at the time because he knew any mention of your name would get his head bitten off.' The ghost of a smile played over his lips. 'But he telephoned your mother — and she said you were in a bad way, depressed and unhappy and totally lacking in all your old sparkle.' Marc gave a harsh little laugh. 'That's when I discovered a side to my brother I hadn't even known existed. He went for me tooth and nail. No,' he went on, seeing the surprised expression in her eyes, 'not physically — but his words were powerful enough! That in itself was a revelation — Ralph's always been afraid to stand up to me. Perhaps that's why he became such a playboy in the first place, because it was the only way he could rebel. But he showed new strengths in standing up for you — and he made sure I knew exactly the sort of person you are. The kind I'd refused to let myself believe in.' His amber eyes held hers. 'He told me about your compassion and your kindness — and your enduring loyalty to him. He also told me you don't like accepting presents. . .' He began walking slowly towards her. 'But I hope you'll accept this one from me.' His rare, devastating smile flashed briefly. 'It was originally intended as a gift for Jersey Zoo. Now it's up to you to decide what to do with it.' Reaching her side he placed a large envelope in her nerveless hands and bent to softly kiss her cheek. 'I'm sorry, Tessa. I hope one day you'll be able to forgive me for everything I put you through.'

She was too shellshocked to move, all the strain of the past few weeks holding her rigidly in place as he walked past her to the door. She wanted to reach out to him, wanted to touch him, yet knew if she did, she'd fall apart all over again.

She heard him talking to her mother for a moment, then the sounds of the front door closing behind him, and it was as if a door had finally closed on her heart, trapping everything within it. Finally forcing herself to move, she stumbled towards the big battle-worn old sofa and subsided into its cushions.

She never knew how long she sat there, staring blindly into space, too numb to make sense of anything. It was only the appearance of her mother, sliding quietly into the room and sitting down beside her on the sofa, that finally broke the spell.

'Are you all right, love?'

'I don't know.' Tessa shook her head, bewildered. 'I don't understand what that was all about. I don't know why he came.'

'He gave you something.' Her mother nodded towards the envelope Tessa was clutching. 'Aren't you going to open it?'

She glanced down in vague surprise, having completely forgotten the envelope's existence. 'I suppose so,' she murmured, but made no move.

'Go on, sweetheart. It must be important, whatever it is.' The hazel eyes were compassionate as she laid a comforting hand on Tessa's arm.

With unsteady fingers she ripped it open and pulled out the contents, her eyes at first confused, then widening in amazement as they skimmed over the paper. At last she looked up, her mouth trembling as she tried to smile, her aquamarine eyes glistening with tears.

'It's incredible,' she whispered. 'I can hardly believe it. He's bought five hundred acres of Brazilian rainforest. And he's given them to me.'

Her mother chuckled softly. 'He obviously realised diamonds wouldn't mean much to you.'

'He said this was originally meant as a gift for Jersey Zoo.' She gave her mother an anguished look. 'Oh, God, Mum, I heard him talking about a Brazilian deal and accused him of being a pirate! I never knew. . .' Then it all became too much for her and she dropped her head into her hands, swamped by tears. Mrs Edwards put her arms around her, murmuring soothing words as the storm of weeping racked her slender body. Then she held her away, her expression gentle but firm as she looked into her daughter's tear-stained face.

'You've been needing a good cry ever since you got here. But there's no need for any more tears, Tess. You've got things to do now. You're going back to Jersey!'

## CHAPTER TEN

TESSA took one last look at herself in the hotel bedroom mirror and chuckled softly. Even her mother's ingenuity in creating goodness knew how many fancy-dress costumes over the years had been stretched with this one. But she'd done a pretty good job. To most people admittedly she'd simply look like a bizarre creature of fantasy, but Marc Duval would recognise the glorious flame and black mane of the golden-headed lion tamarin, one of the rarest and most exquisite creatures at Jersey Zoo, and a victim of the exploitation of the Brazilian rainforests.

The last week had probably been the strangest in her whole life, she mused as she made a last-minute adjustment to the costume, then left the room to join the throng of weird and wonderful characters on their way to take part in Jersey's world-famous Battle of Flowers parade. For once luck had been on her side — the first stroke of good fortune being the discovery that the theme for this year's procession was the animal kingdom. Since then her mother had been sewing frantically, and Tessa seemed never to have been off the phone — making endless surreptitious calls to the highly amused Ralph and Janine, who'd been given the task of finding her a float agreeable to taking an extra passenger on board. More importantly, they'd promised to ensure Marc would be maneouvred into attending the parade.

'Though frankly it won't be easy,' Ralph told her. 'He's been like a bear with a sore head ever since seeing you again. Heaven help any business rivals who tried to get in his way—he'd have eaten them alive!'

'In that case he won't need a costume,' Tessa had laughed, too buoyed up by a faintly fearful excitement to admit the possibility of any last-minute fly getting into the ointment. She was also relieved to hear Ralph sounding so happy and content, clearly enjoying his role as fiancé and solid citizen. His first venture into Marc's business empire hadn't been so terrifying after all, he'd admitted to her—in fact he'd found himself actually relishing the challenge. So he was clearly going to be all right—and suffering not even a trace of the jealousy she'd feared because of her relationship with Marc. On the contrary—he'd thrown himself with glee into the role of conspirator when told of her plan.

As for Tessa, she'd been kept too busy to really think about what she was doing. Now though as she joined the others on the huge and incredible Noah's Ark created entirely from flowers, her stomach muscles clenched in apprehension. Had she read the situation all wrong? Was she about to make a colossal fool of herself? Then she gave a fatalistic little shrug. Things had gone too far now. She couldn't back out. In any case—behind her tamarin mask she smiled ruefully—Geoffrey would never forgive her if she failed to make her leap of faith. She could only hope hers wouldn't end as drastically as his had so many years before.

'The Battle of Flowers' magic has worked again, I see.' A creature bearing a vague resemblance to a giraffe nodded amiably towards her.

'Its magic?'

'Look at that glorious sun up there.' The giraffe neck tilted up towards the clear blue sky. 'It's never let us down in all the long years we've been having the parade.'

'I thought the sun always shone on Jersey,' Tessa returned teasingly, smiling as a bevy of tiny girls trotted by, their long tails and whiskers announcing them as kittens. 'That's what the guide books say!'

'Perhaps not quite always,' the giraffe admitted. 'It just feels that way!'

The procession made its way slowly along the specially cordoned off streets of St Helier, Tessa waving to the crowds thronging the pavements as enthusiastically as all the other participants in their various astonishing creations. Glancing round at some of the other floats in the parade, she could only marvel at the imagination, not to mention the sheer hard graft, which had gone into their making. And it was clearly an event for everyone, she realised with genuine pleasure, spotting quite a number of elderly faces peeping through the animal masks, as well as youthful figures dancing along for the crowd's delight. There was music too, provided by several marching bands as well as musicians on the floats themselves, and she couldn't help but chuckle delightedly as she spotted one group of jazz musicians getting quite carried away as they recreated a scene from the Walt Disney version of *The Jungle Book*, each dressed as an animal character from the cartoon film.

It was a glorious day, a day when islanders came together in a spirit of rivalry and fun as they had done for years, each group trying to outdo the next in the brilliant ingenuity of the flower-decked float. Tessa knew she'd have been thoroughly carried away by the joyful carnival atmosphere of the whole festival—if her breathing hadn't been growing ever more erratic with every moment. As the parade wound its way towards the grandstands set out on Victoria Drive, her heart really went into overdrive. Marc would be there— Ralph and Janine had promised he'd be there. But what if he wasn't? What if some business emergency had kept him away? She swallowed hard as she scanned the crowds frantically, her eyes behind the tamarin mask searching for familiar faces. Then she caught her breath sharply as his dark head came into view.

He seemed strangely detached from the rest, she realised with a pang—a still, remote figure in the midst of all the smiling, cheering crowd. It was now or never. Gathering every shred of courage she possessed, she slipped down from the float and made her way over to the grandstand, nearly tripping over her long tail. He saw her coming, alerted by a nudge in the ribs from Ralph at his side, and a faintly surprised expression crossed his set features.

In all the noise of the parade she knew she hadn't a hope of making her voice heard, so she put on a little mime show, inviting him to join her on the road. At first she thought he'd refuse, his lips thinning in undisguised irritation—then, clearly being urged by Janine, he gave a resigned shrug and clambered his way down. Then he was standing before her, his expression forbidding—until he looked into the aquamarine eyes beneath the flowing golden mane, and his own eyes widened sharply.

'Tessa! Is it you?'

She nodded, unable for a moment to force any words

past the lump blocking her throat. Then she took a deep breath.

'I've come to return the present you gave me,' she said, her voice slightly muffled by the mask. 'Not because I don't want it, but because I trust you with it. I know the forest — and the animals — are safe with you.'

'Is that the only reason you've come back?' The question seemed ripped from him, his voice ragged and harsh.

She shook her head. 'No. I came back because I love you, Marc. I still don't know how you really feel about me, but I believe there's something between us that deserves a chance. If we can stop fighting long enough, that is. Anyway. . .' she gave a soft, breathless little laugh '. . .Geoffrey told me I had to try.'

'Because of your beautiful eyes.' A slow, sure smile carved his mouth, its warmth reaching out to her like a caress. 'Geoffrey wasn't the only one to be driven to madness by a woman,' he said softly. 'I've been in hell since you left. Since I sent you away.' His eyes narrowed warningly. 'But I warn you, Tessa, now that you've come back to me, I'll never let you go again. Can you cope with that?'

She nodded mutely, her heart too full for words. With a groan he enfolded her in his arms and she heard a great cheer erupt around them as the crowds thoroughly enjoyed the unexpected bonus of seeing a Duval pirate claim as his own a golden-headed lion tamarin.

'Are you sure you don't mind missing the night-time parade?' Marc's eyes were tender as he led her into the house and softly closed the door behind them. 'It's really quite spectacular. The floats are lit up and it all turns into quite a party.'

'I don't mind at all,' she returned demurely, feeling a twist of excitement deep within as she looked up into his dark features. The afternoon had been the most wonderful she could ever remember, a feast of laughter and gaiety with Ralph and Janine, and the overwhelming joy of having Marc constantly at her side throughout the festivities. But now she wanted to be with him and him alone. She sent him a teasingly coquettish look from beneath her eyelashes. 'I thought we might have a party of our own. Just the two of us.'

He groaned as he pulled her unresisting form into his arms. 'If you look at me like that, the party might just happen right here in the hallway!'

'Why, Marc! Whatever would Jeanne think?'

'She'd probably be resoundingly grateful that I'd come to my senses at last. The poor woman's been driven half demented by my black moods since you went away.' His arms tightened about her and she thrilled to the possessiveness of his embrace. Then his expression grew serious. 'Are you sure, Tess? I don't want to rush you into anything. If you want more time. . .'

She laid a gentle finger on his lips. 'Do you want me, Marc?' she asked softly.

'Only as a man in the desert wants water!' His eyes closed briefly, then opened again, the amber depths filled with a warm passion. 'Yes, Tessa, I want you. But not only in my bed—I want you in my life. For the rest of my life. I've never said the words to anyone before, but I love you, Tessa.'

She felt the sting of tears behind her eyes, moved

beyond measure by his words. 'And I love you,' she whispered. 'I want to show you how much.'

'Then come with me, sweet lady.' He took her hand in his and led her to his room, barely taking time to close the door before enfolding her against his hard, powerful body. She lifted her face for his kiss, glorying in the new-found freedom to be able to enjoy his caresses with none of the guilt or doubts that had haunted their other passionate encounters.

Inexperienced though she was in lovemaking, she recognised that he was trying to take things slowly, his mouth warm and gentle as it dropped featherlight kisses all over her face. But she was impatient for more, burning up in her need to feel his body against her own, maddened by the barrier of clothes between them. Her fingers went to his shirt, trembling as they undid the buttons and slid the material from his powerful shoulders to reveal a chest lavishly sprinkled with black silky hair. With a moan she dipped her head to his chest, drinking in the warm male smell of him, her mouth glorying in the taste of his skin.

'Dear God, Tessa,' he groaned. 'What are you trying to do to me?' With one easy movement he slipped his arm beneath her knees and lifted her off the floor, crossing the room in a couple of long-legged strides to the bed. There he laid her down, covering her body with his own, swiftly finding the fastenings on her costume and freeing them, his mouth warm and moist as he explored her naked skin below. Somehow their clothes landed on the floor, though she was too caught up in a tempest of fire to know or care how they'd got there. All she knew was the exquisiteness of finally feeling skin against skin, her breasts full and heavy as they pressed against him, her nipples puckering into hard little buds as they begged for his attention. He dropped his head to her breasts, favouring them with his hands and his mouth, his tongue drawing circles, sending ripples of white heat to the very core of her.

His hand slid downwards and she arched helplessly back as his fingers moved with tantalising stealth along her thigh, a tiny whimper torn from her throat as they finally touched the very centre of her longing. Driven by pure instinct, she stroked her hands over his back, her fingers tracing the strength of him, then clutching helplessly as his touch threatened to set her on fire. His hands slid underneath her to bring her closer still to the powerful fullness of his own desire.

'I wanted to make this so good for you, Tessa,' he groaned huskily. 'But you're driving me out of my mind. I need you — now!'

'And I need you.' It was an effort to find her voice, but everything was in her eyes as she gazed into his. 'Make love to me, Marc. Make me yours.'

Then the breath caught in her throat as she felt him push against her, then slide deep into her, a tiny cry escaping her as she felt a flash of pain, then only the deep joy of his possession. Her fingers held to his shoulders as they moved together, caught up in an elemental dance, its rhythm as ancient as time. Then everything seemed to explode like fireworks within her, and she called out his name as she soared to incredible heights, not alone but with him, his arms tight about her as he joined her in flight.

It took a long time to return to earth, her breathing shallow as she clung to him, stunned by the beauty of it all.

'I think I saw shooting stars,' she said at last, when she was once again capable of speech. 'Is it always like that?'

He smiled. 'Only when it's right.' He kissed her forehead. 'And before you start wondering—no, it's never been like that for me before either.' He gazed down at her ruefully. 'I should have followed my instincts the first time I saw you, and whisked you off to bed there and then.'

'Why?' She ran her fingers lovingly through the mat of hair on his chest, smiling in mischievous delight as he caught her hand.

'If you don't stop doing that, you may have to wait a very long time for your answer!' He laid her hand over his heart and she could feel its erratic beat. 'See what you do to me? It's been that way ever since I first spotted you in my garden. But I deliberately convinced myself you were nothing better than a gold-digger because I couldn't cope any other way. If I'd made love to you then, I'd have known I was wrong.' His eyes grew serious as he looked down at her. 'You've never made love before, Tessa. Why not?'

'Because I've never been in love before,' she returned simply. 'And it seems my body can only come to life when it's touched by the man I love.'

'It'll never be touched by anyone else,' he growled, his brows drawing together thunderously. 'I'd kill any man who tried.'

She smiled, revelling in his jealous possessiveness. 'I feel the same way about you and other women,' she admitted, then frowned, struck by a new and unwelcome thought. 'What about Madeleine?'

'What about Madeleine?'

'She gave me a very heavy hint that you and she

were lovers,' Tessa said. 'She more or less said you'd eventually marry her.'

He shook his head. 'Madeleine means nothing to me. I allowed her to store some things here at the house when she sold her own flat.' He grinned wryly. 'And that was a bad mistake—I thought I'd never get rid of her! She kept turning up like a bad penny.'

Tessa felt a second's sympathy for the woman, her own happiness making her wish everyone could be as fulfilled. Then she looked up into his amber eyes. 'What happens now?' she asked hesitantly. 'We lead such different lives. We'll probably spend most of our time at opposite ends of the globe.'

'Is that what you want?'

She shook her head adamantly. 'No.'

'Then it won't happen.' His tone was definite. 'I've been thinking for some time I'd like to become more involved in conservation. After all. . .' he gave a shrug '. . .I've made a great deal of money. More than enough. Perhaps it's time I started giving something back. You can show me how.'

Overcome, she flung her arms round his neck, her eyes filled with tears of joy. 'We can do it together! We can do absolutely anything so long as we're together.'

His eyes gleamed with amber light. 'Absolutely anything?' he queried innocently.

She nodded, a bubble of laughter building up within her. 'Absolutely anything,' she returned solemnly.

'Well, in that case—before we embark on a mission to save the world—I can think of a few other things I'd like us to do together first.'

And he pulled her into his arms to demonstrate exactly what he meant.

# Welcome to Europe

**JERSEY** — 'the honeymoon island'

Imagine fifty miles of beautiful coastline with high cliffs, numerous picturesque bays and harbours, and twenty miles of golden sandy beaches — an island abundant in flora and fauna, from roses to sweet violets, carnations to lavender. Add to this a wealth of historical buildings and places of interest, and people who are welcoming and friendly, and there you have Jersey — a real haven for lovers.

## THE ROMANTIC PAST

Jersey was originally part of Normandy but gained the right to independent government 700 years ago. The island was ruled for 200 years by England after William's conquest but then in 1204, when Normandy was lost to France, the islanders were given the choice of either remaining allied to Normandy or maintaining loyalty to the English Crown. They chose loyalty to England, and since then have enjoyed rights and laws that are subject solely to the Crown, not to the British parliament. Thus to all intents and purposes Jersey is an independent island, although the UK is responsible for the island's defence and international relations.

Jersey has any number of interesting and romantic landmarks and monuments. For example **Bonne Nuit Bay** allegedly got its name when a young man fell from the clifftop, and cried 'Goodnight' to his lover all the way down! Also, **La Rocqueberg** is a large standing stone where young girls used to come for advice from the island's witches — and to ask the names of their future husbands.

One particularly nice marriage custom concerns the island's 'marriage stones'. Newly married couples had their intertwined names carved above the lintel of their homes.

Jersey has a plentiful supply of ghosts, not to mention connections with witchcraft, and even a werewolf — *La Loup Garou*.

The native language of Jersey is a mixture of Norman French and Norse, and is still spoken in some districts. The dialect is called **Jersiais** — people who speak it are known as **Jerriais**. French was the official language until the 1960s, and is still used in the courts and by the legal professions.

Famous people connected with Jersey are **Lillie Langtry** — 'the Jersey Lily'; **Gerald Durrell**, the author and naturalist who set up the Jersey Zoo; **Gilbert**

O'Sullivan; **John Nettles**; **Alan Whicker** and **Harry Patterson** (Jack Higgins).


**THE ROMANTIC PRESENT** — pastimes for lovers. . .

When you arrive in Jersey don't be fooled by the smallness of the island — there is so much scope for sightseeing and activity that you'll be spoilt for choice for things to do. But as well as visiting the host of museums, monuments, castles and manor houses, be sure to make the most of the wonderful unspoilt countryside and scenery too. . .

If you are interested in historical sights — and sites! — there are two impressive castles on the island well worth visiting. **Mount Orgueil Castle** is situated three hundred feet above the pretty harbour of Gorey. Built in the thirteenth century to defend the islanders from the French, it now houses a small museum which provides an insight into the castle's rich history. Venture on to the battlements and you'll be rewarded with a wonderful view of the east coast of the island. **Elizabeth Castle** at St Helier is also well worth seeing, dating from the 1590s, and named by Sir Walter Ralegh, who was Governor of Jersey, after Queen Elizabeth I. The **Militia Museum** and exhibition reveal the part the castle played in the island's history.

Still in the mood for culture? Then head for **Samarès Manor** at St Clement. This is a truly beautiful house set in extensive grounds, with one of the largest herb gardens in Britain. The farmyard is a venue for craft demonstrations and you can take a ride in a Jersey horse-drawn van!

While in Jersey you are bound to be interested in the island's history, so a trip to the **Jersey Museum** is recommended. Here all your questions about the island will be answered in an informative and entertaining way, by means of an audio-visual theatre, exhibitions and an art gallery.

And now, why not spend a few fun-filled hours at the world-famous **Wildlife Preservation Trust and Zoo** at Trinity? Here you can walk through twenty-five acres of water gardens and parkland, and see an amazing collection of the world's rarest birds and animals living in designated areas which have been especially created to resemble their natural habitat.

After all this sightseeing and following the crowds, no doubt you and your partner would like to unwind a little in more peaceful surroundings. . . Perhaps some sunbathing on one of the island's sandy beaches and some swimming in the cool blue sea is what you want, but if you're feeling slightly more energetic there is no better way to savour the island's natural beauty than to take a stroll along one of the several inland or coastal paths, inhaling the scents of the fragrant and colourful flowers and enjoying the tranquillity and lovely scenery. Lovers might also enjoy a visit to the fields of the **Lavender Farm** or the **Butterfly Centre** at Haute Tombette — another 'flowery' place with its own carnation nursery.

Finally, if your visit to Jersey coincides with the second Thursday in August then you're in for a special treat! This is the day of the **Battle of Flowers**, a tradition since 1902, commemorating the coronation of Edward VII and Queen Alexandra. The day was so-called because originally when the carriages paraded through the streets the occupants would throw small bunches of flowers over the spectators. Today the Battle is more like a carnival procession, with each float not only decorated completely in flowers, but also portraying some part of a central theme.

For those of you who appreciate good food, Jersey is the ideal place to indulge yourself! The main culinary specialities are **seafood** — lobster, crab, prawns, oysters, plaice, lemon sole, all cooked to mouthwatering perfection! Those who search may find Jersey cooks still proficient in *La Vieille Cuisine* — old-style cooking, in which case you may sample such delicacies as conger eel soup sprinkled with marigold leaves!

Be sure also to try the island's home-grown juicy **tomatoes**, the renowned **Jersey Royal potatoes**, and of course the inimitable **cream**, **milk** and **butter**. There are also several restaurants on the island that specialise in Italian, Indian, Chinese, Greek, French and even Portuguese and Malaysian cuisine, so you'll have plenty of variety throughout your stay.

With your meal you can sample local wines or cider from the island's own La Mare vineyards, or, if you fancy some local lager, try the award-winning **Mary Ann Pilsner Lager**.

Before you leave Jersey you will surely want some souvenirs to remind you of your stay. St Helier is a great place to shop, with tax-free goods an added incentive to spend, spend, spend! Here you can buy wool sweaters — the world-famous original **'Jerseys'** — or even a **walking stick** made from the stalk of a giant cabbage! Outside St Helier **Jersey Pottery** is the ideal place to purchase all manner of **hand-crafted goods** as well as pottery items.

## DID YOU KNOW THAT. . .?

* Jersey is only fourteen miles from the coast of France and one hundred miles south of mainland Britain.

* Jersey is the largest of the Channel Islands, with an area of forty-five square miles. It is divided into twelve parishes.

* Jersey is an international finance centre; the finance industry is the biggest contributor to Jersey's prosperity. Tourism is its second-largest industry — the island welcomes over a million visitors every year.

* it is estimated that over one hundred and fifty millionaires live in Jersey — approximately three per square mile!

* Jersey's currency is **sterling**, and the island accepts English money and cheques, but the island does have its own coins and notes.

# SUMMER SPECIAL!

**Four exciting new Romances for the price of three**

Each Romance features British heroines and their encounters with dark and desirable Mediterranean men. *Plus, a free Elmlea recipe booklet inside every pack.*

So sit back and enjoy your sumptuous summer reading pack and indulge yourself with the free Elmlea recipe ideas.

Available July 1994          Price £5.70

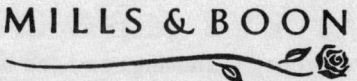

*Available from WH Smith, John Menzies, Volume One, Forbuoys, Martins, Woolworths, Tesco, Asda, Safeway and other paperback stockists. Also available from Mills & Boon Reader Service, FREEPOST, PO Box 236, Croydon, Surrey CR9 9EL. (UK Postage & Packing free)*

# *Full of Eastern Passion...*

Savour the romance of the East this summer with our two full-length compelling Romances, wrapped together in one exciting volume.

**AVAILABLE FROM 29 JULY 1994   PRICED £3.99**

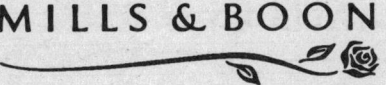

*Available from WH Smith, John Menzies, Volume One, Forbuoys, Martins, Woolworths, Tesco, Asda, Safeway and other paperback stockists. Also available from Mills & Boon Reader Service, FREEPOST, PO Box 236, Croydon, Surrey CR9 9EL. (UK Postage & Packing free)*

# Accept 4 FREE Romances and 2 FREE gifts

## FROM READER SERVICE

Here's an irresistible invitation from Mills & Boon. Please accept our offer of 4 FREE Romances, a CUDDLY TEDDY and a special MYSTERY GIFT! Then, if you choose, go on to enjoy 6 captivating Romances every month for just £1.90 each, postage and packing FREE. Plus our FREE Newsletter with author news, competitions and much more.

**Send the coupon below to:
Mills & Boon Reader Service,
FREEPOST, PO Box 236,
Croydon, Surrey CR9 9EL.**

NO STAMP REQUIRED

**Yes!** Please rush me 4 FREE Romances and 2 FREE gifts! Please also reserve me a Reader Service subscription. If I decide to subscribe I can look forward to receiving 6 brand new Romances for just £11.40 each month, post and packing FREE. If I decide not to subscribe I shall write to you within 10 days - I can keep the free books and gifts whatever I choose. I may cancel or suspend my subscription at any time. I am over 18 years of age.

Ms/Mrs/Miss/Mr _____  EP70R

Address _____

_____

Postcode _____ Signature _____

Offer closes 31st October 1994. The right is reserved to refuse an application and change the terms of this offer. One application per household. Offer not valid for current subscribers to this series. Valid in UK and Eire only. Overseas readers please write for details. Southern Africa write to IBS Private Bag X3010, Randburg 2125. You may be mailed with offers from other reputable companies as a result of this application. Please tick box if you would prefer not to receive such offers ☐